T0283817

Where the Heart Should Be

Where the Heart Should Be

SARAH CROSSAN

Greenwillow Books
An Imprint of HarperCollinsPublishers

Where the Heart Should Be

Copyright © 2025 by Sarah Crossan

All rights reserved. Manufactured in Harrisonburg, VA,

United States of America.

No part of this book may be used or reproduced in any manner whatsoever without written permission except in the case of brief quotations embodied in critical articles and reviews. For information address HarperCollins Children's Books, a division of HarperCollins Publishers, 195 Broadway, New York, NY 10007.

www.epicreads.com

Library of Congress Cataloging-in-Publication Data

Names: Crossan, Sarah, author.

Title: Where the heart should be / Sarah Crossan.

Description: First edition. |

New York, NY : Greenwillow Books, an Imprint of HarperCollins Publishers, 2025. |

Audience term: Teenagers | Audience: Ages Ages 13 up. | Audience: Grades 7–9. |

Summary: During the Great Irish Famine, sixteen-year-old scullery maid Nell falls in love with the wealthy landlord's nephew.

Identifiers: LCCN 2024033443 (print) | LCCN 2024033444 (ebook) |

ISBN 9780063384910 (hardcover) | ISBN 9780063384941 (ebook)

Subjects: CYAC: Novels in verse. | Household employees—Fiction. |

Ireland—History—1837–1901—Fiction. | Romance stories. |

LCGFT: Novels in verse. | Romance fiction. | Historical fiction.

Classification: LCC PZ7.5.C76 Wh 2025 (print) | LCC PZ7.5.C76 (ebook) |

DDC [Fic]—dc23

LC record available at https://lccn.loc.gov/2024033443

LC ebook record available at https://lccn.loc.gov/2024033444

Typography by Paul Zakris

25 26 27 28 29 LBC 6 5 4 3 2

First Edition

Greenwillow Books

Originally published in Great Britain in 2024 by Bloomsbury Publishing Plc

For Aoife

Author's Note

Between 1845 and 1861 one million people died in Ireland of hunger or related diseases, and two million people emigrated from Ireland and never returned. This was triggered by the failure of the potato crop but ultimately caused by the distribution of food across the island of Ireland. At that time, Ireland was a part of the United Kingdom and all decisions regarding its governance were made by politicians in Westminster, London. This story is a work of the imagination. It is an account of a teenage girl living during the Irish famine in a fictional village called Ballinkeel in County Mayo.

Where the Heart Should Be

The Beginning
and the End

Falling

It is hard to tell a love story
and also the story of a people
being torn apart.

But this is what was happening in 1846:
I was falling in love
when everything
around me was
       falling
        down.

I look back with guilt and sorrow
but mostly hope.

Because it is true that love wins.

True love wins
even in the face of death.

And it will guide us.

PART 1
July 1846

The Big House

Maggie Kennedy opens the door,
takes one look at my mucky skirt and boots,
and smacks me flat across the face.
"How dare you come to my door like a dirty pig."

I step back,
   brush myself off.

The dogs behind her
bark and growl,
   teeth bared.

But it's raining,
and standing outside only makes me
   more bedraggled.
"I was clean when I set off, Maggie. I'm sorry."

She lifts her hand to hit me again,
but wipes her thick fingers
on her apron instead.
"My name is Mrs. Kennedy, you cheeky brat.
And I couldn't give a heifer's tit
what you looked like this morning.
You're not to come to this house in that state again.
D'ya hear me?
It's *my* neck on the line
if Lord Wicken sees you in a state."

I nod.

A trickle of summer rainwater
runs
down
my
back.

"Get in here, Nell Quinn."
She grabs my arm and
            drags me into the kitchen,
which is larger than our whole cottage.

I've never been inside
The Big House before.

Maggie gives me a moment to take it in:
the smell of boiling ham and fresh bread,
four large pots burbling on the range,
            their lids tinkling.
In the center of the room is a
                              long table
a bench on either side
and rows of cupboards and shelves
packed with jars of jams and pickles,
        sauces, spices, flour, and sugar.

I've never seen so much food in my life.

My stomach growls.
I only had a small mug
of milk this morning.

Maggie puts her lips to my ear.
"If you pinch so much as a grain of wheat,
the landlord will have you whipped.
And I won't feel one bit sorry.
D'ya understand?"

I nod again.

I understand.
          Whatever is in this house
and within one thousand acres of the grounds
belongs to the landlord,
and we cheat him at our peril.

Maggie hands me a bucket.
"Now scrub that floor you've muddied.
When it's clean, I want it polished.
And tie back your hair like a Christian."

Dog's Dinner

I am on my hands and knees with a brush
while Maggie slices
into steaming cuts of meat.

Greasy scraps fall to the floor.

Before I can get to them,
the fat, growling dogs
have slurped them up.

No one in my home has
had meat since Christmas,
       sweet mutton
       six months ago,
yet here
       in The Big House,
the dogs eat it every day.

Stranger

Sloshing along the muddy lane
on my way home from work,
I catch sight of a stranger walking,

>   his face
>   to the sun.

He is a tall figure.

I watch him   move
        beyond the distant hedgerows.

Who is he,
this person I don't know
in a village where I know everyone
and everyone knows me?

Who is this tall stranger
with his face to the sun?

The Nation

Owen comes tumbling
along the lane
with an armful of nettles rolled in sacking,
        his curls bouncing.
"Do they sleep in gold beds?
Did you have to wipe
their stinking bums for them?"

My brother is ten years old
but tries to imitate the naughty prattle
of older boys.

"I'm a scullery maid.
I won't ever be let out of the kitchen," I tell him.
"Did you work hard at school, Owen?"

He smiles.
"It was so boring I fell asleep.
But Master Sweeney says I'm a genius.
He doesn't care that you left."

"Is that right?"

Owen hands me a newspaper,
a worn copy of *The Nation*,
a gift from the schoolteacher.
        Since I was small, Master Sweeney
        has been offering me things to read,

          pushing me to learn,

          praising me for my memory

     and understanding

         even though

we both knew that at best

I'd amount to nothing more than a servant.

And so I have.

Still,

I turn the pages,

          excited to read

          something new—

              a verse or two.

"He said to give it to Daddy afterwards."

"I know that."

         I read the poems

         and my father follows the politics

             despite Master Sweeney

             passing on the newspaper weeks after

             it's been published,

             once he's read it

             back to front,

             top to bottom.

"Why do you still bother with all that

when you don't have to?" Owen asks.

"Because I like it," I tell him,
and I do, delving into worlds
          and words
that take me away
from Ballinkeel,
          not for long
but a little while.

Owen grimaces.
"It's very suspicious," he says.

Spreading

When we get to the cottage,
my brother drops the nettles in the yard,
calls to Mammy, "Is the dinner made?"

Mammy's washing rags in a bucket,
sitting on a stool beneath the oak tree.
"It's a skivvy he wants," she says.

The heavy rain that came hard and early this morning
stopped all at once in the afternoon,
but there is a light
summer breeze now,
bringing with it the salt of the sea.

The leaves in the oak tree dance above my mother.
"How did you get on up above?" she asks.

"Maggie Kennedy is a pure witch."

"I can believe it," she says.

Owen puts his hands on his hips,
scans our small parcel of land,
      Daddy
      in the middle of it,
his head bent,
examining the lazy beds.
"What's the old man at?" he asks.

My father isn't an old man at all.
He is only thirty-five.
But sometimes I want to look after him.
Look after them all.

"Your daddy's minding his own business, Owen.
Now go and wash your hands," Mammy tells him.

Owen rushes off.

"They're saying the blight's spreading across
the whole country.
From Antrim down to Waterford
and back up to Clare.
He's killed with worry," Mammy whispers.

"Aren't we all," I say.

Mrs. Margaret Kennedy

Slurping his soup,
Daddy says, "If that bitch hits you again,
tell her I'll be up to her with a spade.
I won't have anyone touching my children.
Who does she think she is, anyway?
I knew her when I was a child, Nell.
Her husband was a drunk and a deviant."

Mammy feigns shock. "Michael. Stop that!"

"I will not. It's true.
And I'll have no qualms reminding
Mrs. Margaret Kennedy,
married to Seamus Kennedy,
exactly where she's from
and where she can go to if she isn't careful."

Mammy smiles. "The poor woman
lost her son, Michael; don't be so hard."

Daddy stares. "When? When did she lose her son?"

I didn't know this either.

Owen has his whole face in his bowl.
Suddenly he reappears.
"He went to America last year."

"I thought you meant he died, Mary."
Daddy laughs.

"Well, he's as good as dead to her now.
She'll not see him again."
Mammy is looking at Owen,
her only son.

"That's sad," I say.

Daddy points at me.
"Sad is what Maggie will be if she lays
another finger on you."

Head Down

Once Daddy's out in the yard
           smoking his pipe
Mammy turns to me and says,
"Don't listen to your father.
Keep your mouth shut
           and your head down.
You need that job.
Lord Wicken's calling on your father
less and less for laboring work.
He's had nothing from him in a month."

Then
more gently, "Get yourself to bed now.
You've to be up again at dawn."

"I promised Rose I'd go up to the hill to see her."

Mammy frowns.
"Couldn't she have carted her pretty rear end
down here?
She knows you're working."

"I won't be long, Mammy. I promise."

Up on the Hill

Rose McElligott and Eamon Flynn
are by the well,
shouting into it,
listening to the sounds of their own voices
echoing back at them.

> I have known them both for so long
> and Rose since I was born—
> the two of us coming into the world in the
> same week,
>> to mothers who were themselves
>> best of friends since infancy.

"Come and dance, Nell!" Rose shouts.
She takes Eamon's hands and they spin
around and around in the gloaming.
Then, howling,
they fall over in a fit of giggles
and paw at one another,
eventually dragging themselves over to me.

But they can't keep their hands off each other.
> Or their lips.

"Watching you is exhausting," I say.
"I prefer it when you hate each other."

"Don't worry,
we're due a breakup soon," Eamon says,
and I believe him.

The two of them are always
        heating up,
        cooling down,
        breaking up,
        breaking down,
        and finally getting back together.

Their romance is as
repetitive as Sunday Mass.

"How's The Big House?" Eamon asks.

"Pure heaven. They treat me like a princess," I say,
showing them my palms, blistered from a full day
of scrubbing stone floors and dirty pots.

"Well, at least you don't live in the house
like some of them.
Can you imagine?" Rose says.

"You'd end up with an accent like Queen Victoria."

"At least you *have* work," Eamon adds.

"I know that. I'm not complaining."

"My uncle Paddy took his family
to the workhouse in Ballina last week," he says.
"I couldn't think of anything worse."

No one speaks for a few moments
because we've all heard about
the horrors of the workhouse:
families torn apart,
their bodies deloused.
            Many people who go in never come out,
                    though some do leave—
                    abandoning their own
                    children once they realize
                    the promise of porridge isn't
                    worth the degradation
                    of the place.

"I'm going to save some money
and leave Ballinkeel.
Go to London maybe," I say. "Or America."

I'm not sure this is true
            or even what I want
but if the rumors about the rot are true, then
it's a sensible goal: get out of Ireland.

Eamon lies on his back.
"Me too," he says. "We can't stay here.
There's nothing for us."

"Am I nothing?" Rose asks, tickling him lightly.

He shrugs. "You know what I mean."

"I don't," she says. "I never want to leave Mayo."

"Never?" Eamon asks. "That's a very long time."

Rose sits up straight, presses her full lips together
until they are almost invisible.
She frowns too—
      scrunching up her elegant features
      for full effect
      so she seems almost ugly.
This is what happens to my best friend's face
whenever Eamon has annoyed her.
"So you'd just leave me, would you?"

"Would you not want to come with me?" he asks.

And this is how their breakups start:
a harmless conversation turning into something
heavy until
Rose makes me referee,
      knowing I have to take her side.
But I haven't the energy for it.
"Don't fight tonight," I plead. "I'm tired.
Tear ribbons out of one another tomorrow instead."

Change in the Weather

I've fallen asleep on the grass and
wake up to Rose shaking me.
"It's gonna lash.
Come on!" she says,
          and hurtles down the hill with Eamon.
"Come *on!*"

I sit up,
legs stiff and sore.
Mammy was right. I should have gone
straight to bed after dinner.
The wind groans.
And so do I.
"Wait!" I shout. "Rose!"

But I am alone.

And I haven't the strength
          to race after them.

Loitering

At the crossroads
someone is loitering,
listening to my friends' retreat,
watching them charge away.

He is tall and wearing a neat, blue blazer.
His hair is as black as Tipperary coal
       and tousled by the storm.

"They went that way," he murmurs,
                      pointing.

Something in his composure
      as he speaks
makes me stumble.

And stop.

Plus,
he is English.

I know straightaway
that he is the stranger I saw walking.

"Who are you?" I ask.

"I'm John Browning," he says carefully,
like the name might mean something.
"And you are?"

"My name is Ellen Quinn. Nell."

"Well, you better be quick, Nell,
or you won't catch them.
And it looks like worse rain is on the way."

"I'm taking a different road than them," I say.
"I'm going in the opposite direction."

I wait,
            wanting something.

            I can't think what it is.

Behind him,
smoke from the fire of home
snakes into the slate-gray sky.

He scans the roads.
"You're alone.
Are you not afraid?"

"Only a little bit," I say.

The Terrible Storm

Mammy is waiting at the cottage door.
"I was starting to fret," she says.

"I fell asleep on the grass," I tell her.

The window creaks in its hinge.
The roof rattles.

Mammy screams and grabs Owen,
pressing him to her chest.
"Get off me, Mammy!" he complains.

But she won't.
She squeezes her eyes shut, holds on tighter.
"It's the banshee!
I'd know that wailing anywhere.
My granny died on a night like this.
Can you hear her keening?"

"It was gusty up on the hill," I say.
I have to raise my voice against the storm.

My skirt and stockings are drying,
     dripping over the fire
     making it
     pop and sizzle.

For some reason I haven't
mentioned the Englishman I met.

        The boy.
John Browning.

"You'd never know it was summer," Daddy says,
unlatching the door to look out.
He laces up his boots.
"You rest yourself, Mary.
I'll go and see what's making that racket."

"Do not. You'll be torn apart
by the gale!" Mammy shouts.
"I saw the banshee when I was expecting Owen.
Do you remember, Michael?
She was no taller than a child.
But her face was wizen. White.
I was petrified I'd lose him."

Beyond the cottage
something *is* caterwauling,
a siren spinning in the thunder.
                A noise I've never heard before.

My mother leaps up,
sprinkles our possessions with holy water—
liberally splashing some at us,
as well as at the goat in the corner
and the chickens clucking by the door.
"This water was blessed by the bishop
when he was in Killala last week," she says.

Daddy kisses her forehead.
"That's enough, Mary."

"The crops, Michael," she whispers.

Daddy gently takes the holy water from Mammy,
about to head up to our field to protect it.

But as he does,
        the banshee's screams disappear
        and the rain stops.

Just like that.

The world falls silent.

After the Storm

My father is digging the field
       behind the house.
"He's been up all night," Mammy says.
"We'll have no spuds in the ground come October,
with his picking and poking."

"How many have we left from last year?"

Mammy shakes her head: we have none.

Our hens peck at pebbles.
The hot air hardly moves.

"I have to get to work," I tell her.

"Good. Go on now. Don't be late."

All Day

I scrub pots and pans
with my bare hands,
the water either scorching or icy cold.

Maggie stirs soups,
kneads bread.

Occasionally she pops
a piece of cheese
or a small bun
into her mouth.
She thinks I'm not watching,
but when she sees I am she shouts:
"You don't get paid to gawk."

A Decent Dinner

My wages are to be paid
at the end of every week,
but each day
       as part of my service
            and to keep me working hard
I get a small plate of dinner.

Maggie serves up two potatoes
and chopped carrots,
a cube of butter melting
on top of them
the same as yesterday.

I stare down at the meal.

"Was it venison you were hoping for?" she asks.
"Get it into you."

Meat for the dogs
and spuds for the servants.

Naturally.

Long Story

I am ready to go home,
opening the back door
and stepping into the yard,
when John Browning
appears in a pair of riding boots.
"Oh. Pardon me," he says awkwardly,
                    and steps aside.

His trousers are muddy,
his face flushed.

He must live here.
        Of course.
        Where else?

As I close the door
it comes into my head
that I should curtsy, and nervously
    I do,
though I know it's unnecessary and stupid.
    He blinks, shakes his head,
    and waves away the gesture.
"I believe we met last night," he says,
as though I could have
forgotten
running into a fine-looking
English stranger.

"Yes, sir," I say. "We did."

"You've got a decent sprint on you.
One moment you were there;
the next you were gone."
He smiles, holding out his hands
palms to the sky
in a gesture of benign confusion.

I am expected to answer,
but I doubt he wants me to engage him
in a real conversation.
"I had to get home quickly, sir.
I wasn't running away."
I am servile
and hate the sound of my own voice
    as I speak,
my deference to this
boy who is my own age.

"I've not seen you on the estate before."
His voice has become a little lofty,
    perhaps in response to my reserve.

"I started working here yesterday, sir.
I'm the new scullery maid."

"Oh. I see."
He begins to unbuckle his boots
        and talks into the ground.
                I stand still.
"I arrived myself from London two weeks ago.
Philip Wicken is my uncle.
I came across with my sister's husband.
    He's gone home again.
Not that you asked for my life story."

Is it an interesting story? I want to ask.
        But why?
        Who is he to me?
        Who could he ever be?
"I hope you will be happy here, sir," I say stiffly,
owning my place in the pecking order.

He pulls off the boots,
bangs the soles together,
and unbuttons his jacket.
"I'm not sure about happy, but I'll certainly
be kept busy."

I move away from the door,
and to my surprise he opens it,
going into the house
the same way the servants would.

Rotten

A few days after the storm,
news begins to spread like dandelion clocks
that Mayo is in for it:
a black poison has been found in the potatoes,
a putrid smell coming from most of the crops.

I thought we had escaped the blight
this year
          like we did last year.
I thought we were the lucky ones.

But no.

The stories are true.

Slimy black potatoes,
       like overgrown slugs,
          are scattered across our lazy beds.

The smell draws sick from my stomach.
There can be no mistaking.
"The potatoes are mush," Daddy mutters.

"Ruined," Owen adds. "I planted these myself."
He is on the verge of tears.

Daddy puts an arm around him.
"Go on down, son.
Help your mother with the supper."

"Can nothing be saved?" I ask Daddy
once Owen is out of earshot.

He kicks a pile of potatoes
that don't look too bad.
"We'll boil up those ones."

"We have the oats.
They're in good shape," I say.

In the distance
        the oats sway golden
        against the stench.

"Once they're sold,
we'll just about afford the rent
and then we've got nothing.
As soon as they're harvested,
Wicken will want his money."
Mammy waves at us using both hands.

"What will we do?" I ask my father.

He sniffs.
"I was about to ask you the same question."

A Secret

Rose and I shoo birds from the lane.
"How was your crop?" I ask.

"Slop," she says. "I saw my da sobbing.
I've never seen him do that.
I prefer it when he's furious."

"Mammy keeps blaming the banshee," I tell her,
rolling my eyes.

"Or the fairies. I mean,
it wasn't Our Lady, was it?" Rose says.

I am surprised by Rose's superstition.
"There has to be a logic to it.
Daddy says the beds are diseased."

"Nell, didn't the sky darken
that night we were up on the hill?
          Like a turf pit.
And the wind and the noise.
That wasn't thunder.
It was the fairies fighting.
Mammy said we should have
left gifts outside for the good people."

"But the rot's everywhere. Last year too.
They're writing about it in the newspapers.
Even the English ones."

"And you believe the English, do you?"
Rose looks at me like I should be hanged
        for treachery.

So I say nothing about running into
John Browning
even though Rose is my best friend
and I am desperate to mention him to someone,
just to say his name out loud.

Not that there's much to say.

Twice
we have exchanged polite remarks.

                        That is it.

John Browning and I have spoken
like two strangers sometimes do.

But it *is* a sort of secret
or a bit of juicy gossip at least,
        the sort I would normally share with Rose.
Because he is from The Big House
and not like the rest of us.

And certainly
not like me.

Stench

We cannot stay in the cottage,
      are forced
      into the yard,
where we cover our noses
      with cupped hands.

The boiled bits of spuds
we thought were safe
stink,
are full of slime.

"The storm," Mammy says. "And that sly banshee."

Daddy kicks the dirt and says,
"The whole lot's for burning."

          Mountains of potatoes
      in neighboring fields
are rotting,
      oozing their way into
early graves.

A cluster of men gather together,
      caps in hand,
      scratching their heads.
Daddy walks up the lane to join them.

Night comes and Mammy says,
"It'll be onion soup for tea."

She stirs a pot
                and the sour smell
                wafts through the cottage.
"I put a bit of pepper into it.
It's lovely and hot."

Onion soup we hate,
yet no one complains
because now we know
there's nothing as bad
as a cursed
                black
                potato.

At the End of the Week

Maggie counts out
one shilling and sixpence
for the work I have done this week,
the coins stacking up
in my hand like a
trim
silver
tower.

It won't buy us much,
certainly couldn't cover a fraction of the rent
in a few months,
but along with the hens' eggs and
few vegetables we have left,
it'll stop us heading to the workhouse.

For a while.

Daddy says, "Well done, Nell,"
and takes the money from me shyly.
"I'll head up to Killala tomorrow
and see what's for sale."

He smiles proudly,
but beneath it I know there is shame:
his daughter
is now feeding
the family.

Summers Before

Maggie wasn't always the cook
at The Big House.
Daddy's old aunt, Sally-Maeve,
was in charge of Wicken's kitchen
until she died a few years ago,

And sometimes,
when Daddy was up on the estate
doing jobs for the landlord,
Sally-Maeve would slip him fruit or biscuits
from the previous night's supper
if he promised to tell no one where he got them.

Daddy would take us to the bay
and we would paddle in the shallows
while Mammy screamed, "Be careful!"
Then we'd picnic
on Mammy's potatoes and buttermilk
and Wicken's sweet leftovers.

No chance of that now.

Not with Maggie as gatekeeper to Wicken's kitchen
and the potatoes turned to slop.

Heir

To escape the steam of the kitchen
I am eating
outside,
      sitting on the stone steps.

As well as the potatoes,
Maggie has given me a splinter of burned bacon,
which I've already
slipped into my apron
to take home to Owen.

Across the yard I spot Lord Wicken
and his nephew examining the estate,
Wicken pointing,
John Browning nodding
but not really looking,
      his eyes a little glazed over.

A new wing is being built,
which Maggie says will be used
as a private chapel.
Also a burial vault has been planned
and further outbuildings for more pigs.
Four or five men from Ballinkeel busy themselves
digging foundations, and
I wonder whether this project will mean
work for my father.

Lord Wicken and John Browning
turn and head in my direction.

Neither of them makes eye contact
even when they are so close
I can hear them speaking.

> I lower my gaze,
>> wonder whether
>> John Browning notices me.

"I need to focus on modernizing the holdings,"
Wicken is saying.
"We'll saddle up and I can show you where I plan
to clear the land for cattle.
Ultimately what happens to the land
becomes an issue of economics."
> I look up as they pass by,
> wondering what he means by this,
>> whether modernizing the land
>> will impact his tenants.
> Neither of them condescends to acknowledge me.

Wicken continues,
"If you effectively oversee this building work
it will go some way to proving
I've not made a mistake in naming you my heir."

"I understand, sir."
He addresses his uncle
using the same tone a servant might take.

And yet he is to inherit Wicken's estate,
which makes sense.
Wicken has no sons.
His wife died the year they married,
leaving him with no children at all.

This bequest by Wicken to his nephew
is more gossip
that I would normally share with Rose
        and maybe even Mammy and Daddy,
            but I'm not sure I can.

            And for some reason
            I'm not sure I want to.

Doctor Riley

Owen saunters across the yard.
"Doctor Riley's dead," he says casually,
like he's reporting on a game of hurling.

"What happened to him?" I ask.

"Took sick.
He had blood in his shite for a week beforehand.
And his wife's on her way out too.
The snobby bitch."

"Owen!" I cuff him around the head.

"What? He did die, and she is dying.
        I'm not lying."

"Don't mention the doctor," I tell Owen.
"Mammy and Daddy have enough worry."

But Owen can't keep his mouth
shut for five minutes
and blabs about Doctor Riley
and his sick wife
as soon as Mammy asks
for news.
Daddy scratches his head.

"It's just the beginning," he says.
"Believe me."

And I do.

I believe it is just the beginning.

PART 2

August 1846

Shelley and Coleridge

I bump straight
        into him as I rush from the kitchen
with a pot of soapy water
and soak him entirely.
"Damn it!" he mutters,
looking down at his drenched trousers.

"I'm so sorry, Master Browning."
I place the pot on the ground
and pull a cloth from
the band of my skirt.
He doesn't take it.

He crouches to pick up something:
        my book,
                a tatty collection of poems
                by Shelley
loaned to me by the schoolteacher.
It must have fallen from my pocket
as we collided.
"You read?" he asks.

"We aren't all illiterate, sir," I say sharply
and regret it immediately.

He looks up, surprised,
though whether it's my tone that's shocked him
or my ability to read
I do not know.

"I haven't read Shelley.
My tutor liked Coleridge.
He was a bit of a maverick.
Thank God that's all over with."
He hands back the book.

"Shall I get you a clean towel, Master Browning?"

He looks down at himself,
         remembering.
"I can take care of it myself. Thank you."

I lift the pot and return to the kitchen.

I am shaking slightly.

Damn it.

Champagne

The next day
several heavy crates are unloaded from a cart
and carried down to the cellar.

Maggie watches without comment,
her mouth tight.

"Is it wine?" I ask William Gaughan, the footman.

"Champagne," he whispers, nudging me.
William is a thin man, around my father's age,
with hair slicked down to one side and a very
straight back.
He is from Ballinkeel
        but has lived in The Big House a long time,
        has a soft accent that's not easy to place.
"Six cases of champagne from France
via Liverpool via Dublin.
Imagine.
I'd kill for a bottle
and drink the lot myself straight from the neck."

"You would not."

He winks. "I might."

I roll the word around in my mouth—
        champagne—
and even the smooth flavor of
those sounds
tastes good.

Six cases of champagne. Imagine.

All the World's Secrets

Owen tells a story
about a sparrow
that came to him in the night and told him
All the Secrets of the World.

"Was this a nightmare?" Daddy asks,
         not much interested.
He taps his pipe against the sole of his boot.
Tobacco peppers the floor of the cottage.

Owen shakes his head.

"What were the secrets?" I ask.
I keep my tone light,
but I would actually like to know—
any hint at all would be a help.

Owen shakes his head again.
His curls are all knotted.
"I can't tell *all* the world's secrets," he says.

Mammy coughs, sits back, pushes damp
         strands of hair from her face.
"Well, at least tell us what's polluted the potatoes."

Mass

Rose raps on the cottage door.
"Are you coming to Mass?" she asks.

"At a halfpenny each we'll stay at home
and pray for a while," Daddy says,
       stoking the fire.
"Can't be wasting money after that harvest."

Mammy says, "It's a disgrace, Father Liam
still asking for money during days like this.
                  The neck on him."

"I'll walk you there, Rose," I say,
slipping on Mammy's old boots.
Each Sunday I am permitted the morning off
to attend Mass;
           I should at least look like I'm going.

The day is dry, the sun bright.

Rose links my arm and at the turn in the road says,
"I have to go to Mass or Father Liam
might not agree to marry Eamon and me."

"You're getting married?"

"I hope so.
I was with him last night and we . . ."
        She squeezes my wrist.

"Rose, you didn't.
The last thing you need is a baby.
Your dad would kill him."

I think about all the times
as young girls
Rose and I talked about liking boys,
kissing them,
not understanding what came next
but knowing you didn't do it in public,
that you had to hide and
even pretend not to want it.
"What was it like?" I ask.

Rose considers the question.
"It was a bit sore."

She has done it all,
might be married soon,
and although we've been friends
our whole lives I feel embarrassed
suddenly
                and strangely
                small.

"Do you want a coin to get into church?" she asks.

I look at her palm,
           a halfpenny resting in its center.
"No, you should keep it.
I don't remind Rose that her family
has more mouths to feed than mine
and no one in her home
has a job.

"You'll find someone, Nell," Rose says,
like romance is the most important thing in the world.
She kisses my cheek and skips into Mass.

I stand outside.

I can hear some of the sermon.

I can hear some of it even
standing
           outside.

But it's not really the same.

Seven Courses

Maggie and I work from the ink of morning
until the black of night
preparing a meal of seven courses for
Lord Wicken and his six guests
who arrive in two carriages
pulled by horses.

I have never seen some of the foods before,
nor so much piled onto plates
and left uneaten:
pickled salmon and quails,
rabbits with red onions,
beef steaks,
cheesecakes,
Dutch cheese,
and orange butter.

Such abundance
and waste
while many of his tenants' children
are already withering away.

After Dinner

I am heading down the driveway
after the fancy banquet
when I see John
by the iron gates.
He is leaning against them,
doing nothing in particular.

I slow my pace,
hoping he'll move away,
hoping he'll stay.

When I get closer he
squints against the gloom.

"Sir," I say. "Good evening."

In his hand he is holding an empty wineglass
upside down
by its stem.
"What time is it, Nell?" he asks.

"I'm not sure, sir."

"Have the guests gone to bed?"

"I don't know," I say.
I wish I knew something.
I'm sure I sound like a dolt.

"Major Chambers is spouting all kinds of tosh
about . . . Well, it doesn't matter what it's about . . .
but it's like being lectured at by a foghorn," he says.

I hide a smile.
Even from the kitchen
we could hear Major Chambers
remonstrating against the weather, his gout,
Irish peasants, and the workhouses.

"Was it a pleasant evening, sir?"

"The food was lovely, thank you," he says.

"I wasn't looking for a compliment, sir," I say,
        though being given one
        feels good.

"People usually call me Johnny."
He takes a step toward me
and instinctively I step back,
afraid of something happening inside me,
but not afraid of him.
        The clouds have covered the sickle moon.
        It is very dark.

"Can I do anything for you, sir,
before I go home?" I ask,
not sure what else to say.
I am finished for the day
and have no intention of going back up
to The Big House.

He shakes his head.
"Johnny. Please.
Would someone here just use my name?
Would you?"

A Name

Sir.
Master Browning.
Master John.
John Browning.
Johnny Browning.
Johnny.

Just use my name,
he says.

Like We Were Familiar

And if I did
use Johnny's name,
casually,
>> like he and I were familiar,
>> and someone overheard me—
>>> Maggie
>>>> or Wicken—
what then?

Sissy Doyle

Our neighbor Sissy Doyle died yesterday—
lay down and never got up.
"Didn't I say the doctor was only the beginning?"
Daddy says. "Didn't I tell you?"

I saw Sissy at the well
not long after I started working at The Big House
but hunger took her,
      they say,
            pure and simple.
Now there are seven children
and no mother over at her place.

"Half the potato crop in Ireland has failed and
what is that new prime minister doing about it?
Or the landlords?"

"Try not to get upset, Michael," Mammy says.

But Daddy has been upset for a long time.
He's read the newspapers and knows:
"They're doing nothing at all
either over here or over there.
I'm telling you, I swear to God,
it's a great hunger that's coming
across the whole island
and a few soup kitchens won't be enough to
save us."

Mammy holds Daddy's hand but
even that doesn't silence him.
"We live in the richest goddamn
empire in the world.
Do you think they'd allow this to happen
in England?" he shouts.

Mammy finally takes in what my father is saying.
"You're right, Michael.
But what can we do about it?"

Daddy doesn't have an answer.

And then, even though we have little to spare,
Mammy says, "Keep an eye on Owen, Nell,"
and stalks off to deliver a few onions
to Sissy Doyle's house
so those poor seven won't starve.

Not today anyway.

A Visit from the Priest

The priest is at the door looking dour.
Mammy ushers him inside,
offers him the best seat.
"You're very welcome, Father," she says.

"Thank you, Mrs. Quinn.
I know I am. I know yous are decent people."

Mammy holds her head high,
                              elongates her back.

"So I was surprised not to see yous at Mass.
Was there a sickness on you?"

He must be able to smell the stinking fields
          from the cottage,
          must know we lost our crop.

Mammy pours him a tea.
"We've decided to save our money for food, Father.
We've had hard decisions to make."

He refuses the drink.
"Saving money won't save your souls."

Mammy almost grins.
"I'll be sure think about that, Father."

The priest startles like she has sworn at him.
"I should hope you will think about it.
We've a greater need for God than ever before."

Mammy holds her ground.
        Watches him.
"If only it were cheaper to worship him."

"Good day to you, Mrs. Quinn."

An Audience with Wicken

Daddy paces the yard
      back and forth
      muttering to himself.

Inside, Mammy is stirring a pot of
something watery.
I take over from her and she sits down
with a sigh.
"Gilly McElligott said Wicken still wants his rent
but they can't pay it.
The landlord wouldn't
evict anyone, would he?" she asks.
"It isn't just them. Half the tenants won't have
anything but the money from the oats,
and most of them will spend that money on food.
The landlord isn't an evil man. Is he?"

"I don't know, Mammy.
But at least he's in Ireland and not in England
leaving everything to someone else."

"That's true. He's involved with the people here.
He *must* care about us in some measly way."
I nod but don't tell her what I overheard a few
weeks ago:
Wicken talking to his nephew about clearing
the land for cattle.
      It may have meant something.
      It may have meant nothing.

"Would you have a word
with him if you do run into him, Nell?
Would you explain for us?
He's always got on well with your father
and you've a good way with words.
He'll listen to you."

Again I nod,
    because
I don't know how to tell my mother
what it's like for me at work:
I'm invisible to Lord Wicken
        so it's unlikely
I'll be getting an audience
with him any time soon
even if his nephew
has stooped so low as to speak to me.
"I need to talk to Daddy," I say,
to hand over my meager
weekly wages again.

But when I go into the yard,
my father has gone
back up to the field
to study the land
that has betrayed him.

Two Weeks

I can hear Rose singing before I reach
    the brim of the hill.

Eamon waves me over, tries to pass me his pipe.
"God, no," I say, pushing away his hand.

It is a bitter night.
He wraps an arm around me
like we might be lovers.
    I let it linger.
        Know it's a safe place to sit.

Rose holds her final note a long time.
We clap loudly.
Then she holds up a bottle
and that gets a louder round of applause from us.
"Cleanse our souls, Holy Father."
She takes a slug—it isn't her first.

I take a sip myself.
It catches in my throat.
I cough.
But it tastes less brittle than the usual stuff
they stumble across.
"Where did you get the drink?" I ask.

"I did some laboring for Murphy.
His daughter took a shine to me," Eamon says.

Rose hums to herself, her head in
          Eamon's lap.
"But Eamon loves me the most," she says.
"So we're getting married in two weeks and
Sheena Murphy can go to hell.
Daddy's given his blessing.
Mammy's asked Father Liam,
who is less keen than we'd like,
but who gives a hoot about him?"

Rose is sloshed, so I'm not sure she's serious.
"Are yous really?"

"Really," Eamon says.

"In two weeks?"

"Why not?" Rose says.

I hug them
          but cannot speak for a few moments.

What will I do once my best friend is a wife?
          We won't be coming up
to the hill to drink, dance, and sing
when they've shackled themselves to one another,
that's for sure.

"You're getting married in two weeks," I repeat.
I tug on Rose's skirt to get her attention.

"I am." She beams.

"We are," Eamon says solemnly.
"And we might build a cottage behind
my father's place to live in."

"Congratulations," I say quietly.

It is as much enthusiasm as I can muster.

Respectable

"They make a beautiful couple," Mammy says.
"Gilly is absolutely delighted.
And to think she was worried Eamon would slip off
to America or Liverpool
and then what would her Rose be good for?"

"Mammy, don't talk like that," I say.

Mammy waggles a finger at me,
a kind of warning, maybe:
"You can't be married if everyone knows
you were out walking with a boy.
She isn't in the family way, is she?"

"No, Mammy!" I feign shock
because Rose could very well be carrying a baby
and not even know it herself.

"Of course she isn't.
But you know,
sometimes girls get into trouble
when no one's looking,
and then she'd have no choice but to get married.
Eamon Flynn is a good boy.
I don't think he'd take advantage."
She nudges me. "It'll be you next, Nellie."

I find the latest edition of *The Nation*
sent over to us by the schoolteacher,
          open it in the middle,
and ignore my mother.
Sometimes she talks so much
it's better to let her blather on
without contradicting her.

But I don't like what she's saying.

I don't like so much of what she's saying.

Time Enough

When I replay my discussion with Mammy,
Daddy says, "Don't listen to your mother.
        Each to his own.
And you've time enough for that kind of carry-on."

Carry-On

The kind of carry-on
Mammy means is marriage.
The kind of carry-on
Daddy means is love.

But how do I know
how much time I have left for those things?
Everything is expiring
before it should.

And anyway,
maybe I'm ready for some carry-on
now.

Maybe
that kind of carry-on
is exactly what I want.

Percy Shelley

The laborers are taking a break,
eating porridge from tin bowls.

He is close to them
   but also noticeably apart,
leaning against
a stone outbuilding
where a sow is spending
her days and nights feeding
eight ravenous piglets.

I move toward him slowly,
holding the ends of my apron
   heavy with peelings,
and hoping he will look up
before I reach him.

But he is reading a book,
his mouth moving as his eyes
   shift left to right.
The book is red
with gold lettering
and on the front
a name:
Percy Bysshe Shelley.
I clear my throat and he startles,
holds the book by his side.

"I won't disturb you.
I've just brought peelings for the pig."

"You aren't disturbing me."

I take the peelings to the sow,
throwing them into her trough.
"Eat up now, Hetty."
She grunts and wriggles,
though stays lying on her side,
pale gray piglets lined up along her mottled body.

I don't speak as I leave,
don't even look at him,
but once I am back by the kitchen door
I glance quickly in his direction
and he is watching me.

I am glad.

Wedding Day

The whole village is twirling in time
to the fiddler's tunes,
　　　up and down the crossroads
　　　all night long to celebrate
Rose and Eamon's wedding.

The couple looks so happy,
like the world was created just for them.

"They're playing your song!" Rose calls.
She is mocking me.
A running joke between us:
They're playing your song, we say to one another.
I don't even remember what it means.

I shake my head.
"Dance with your husband!"

"My husband!" she shouts.
"My husband? Oh, God."

Eamon spins Rose so fast
I'm sure she'll be sick if he doesn't let go.
　　　But he does
and Rose's father, Bobby,
takes his chance to reclaim her,
to hold his daughter tight to his chest.

I want to celebrate,
be happy for my best friend,
but all I feel is alone,
like the happiness
they have found in one another
will never find *me*.

The Hens

Owen strokes
the brown hen in his arms.

"Come on. They aren't pets," I remind him.
"And she's stopped laying eggs."

> All three of them have stopped,
> for weeks now.
> And every day there is less and less
> meat on them.

"I love them."

"It's one of the hens or Gertie," I tell him.
Owen gasps, drops the hen,
and rushes across to our goat.
"Wouldn't you like some meat?" I ask.

"Why can't you get it from The Big House?"

"Because it would be stealing, Owen.
I'd lose my job and maybe my head."

"Poor Gertie," Owen whines,
stroking her bristly head.

The brown hen pecks away
at dirty potato skins in the yard,
unaware her days are numbered.

I suppose that's better, though.

Who'd want to know
                    death was around
                    the corner?

Much better to be in the dark.

Much better to be pecking one day
and dead the next
than constantly worrying about
when your master
was about to wring your neck.

Much better to be in the dark.

By Nightfall

By nightfall two hens are dead already,
lying
   on their backs in the dust—
     anchored there,
   twiggy legs pointing upward
   like broken signposts.

Daddy isn't the one who killed them.
It must have been the rank spuds that did it:
if they were too rotten for us to eat,
we should have known the birds
couldn't digest them,
and with their brains as small as they were,
they were too stupid to realize.
I was stupid too:
I should have brought the hens
the carrot peelings from The Big House
once we ran out of our own scraps.

If we'd wrung their necks earlier
we'd have had a feast tomorrow,
but we can't eat hens that died of poison,
already dead and
   decomposing in the dirt.

Owen says, "We should bury them."
He is trying hard not to snivel.

I squeeze his small hand,
thinking only of the waste.

Daddy throws the hens
        beyond the wall into the field.

Carrion crows circle the sky.

The remaining white hen clucks and worries.
I am moved by her perseverance,
        the way she clings to life
despite what happened to the others.

I know
        she doesn't deserve death.

"Go inside, Owen," I say,
and once he's in the cottage
I yank the hen
from the ground by her legs
and in one swift
crack
wring
her neck.

"Dinner," I say aloud
to no one.

Soupy

We eat the last of the chicken,
sending a bit of meat up to the McElligotts,
who offer us a few herring in return.

Slowly Daddy stirs his soup,
staring into its murky depths.

"We'll be fine," I tell him.
"And next year the crop will thrive."

Owen hiccups,
     a popping sound
     so cute you'd be mad not to smile.
"I'm full up," he says.

"Eat your soup," Daddy snaps.
"Every last lick of it."
He does not hit my brother
but his hand is raised.

Daddy stares at the hand, shocked.
"Eat your soup, son," he soothes.

Alone in The Big House

He has been left alone
to manage the building works at The Big House
while Lord Wicken goes to Belfast on business.

William Gaughan serves Wicken's nephew
his meals in the dining room
and reports back:
>"The poor lad looks lost," he says,
>shaking his head
>>like it is a terribly sad thing
>>to eat lavish meals
>>all alone.

One morning,
>early,
John Browning wanders into the kitchen
in his bare feet.

I am stirring a pan of scrambled eggs with cream
for his breakfast.

Maggie pushes loose strands of her gray hair
into her cap. "Sir," she says, "I'm so sorry
if you're having to wait.
Breakfast won't be long."

He looks along the shelves
as though searching for something.
"Did any letters arrive from my sisters?"

"I have no idea, sir. I don't deal with the deliveries.
William will be better able to help you."

"Understood," he says, and then seems to see me.
"Good morning, Nell. You're here early."

"I'm here every day at this hour except Sundays, sir."

Maggie glances between us,
but my eyes are back on the slimy eggs.
        If they burn, Maggie will smack me
        and I'll have to recook them.

"And no news on my uncle's return?" he asks.
"He said he'd be back yesterday."

Maggie frowns like she is confused by the question
and I'm sure she is:
we are not notified about the comings and goings
of Lord Wicken.
It is his home and he does as he pleases.
Often he skips meals
we have spent hours cooking
or demands extra place settings for guests
        with no notice at all.
"I've not heard anything, sir," Maggie says carefully.

He steps toward me. Peers into the pan.
"I'll take my breakfast in my bedroom today,"
he says.
"As a treat. Since it's my birthday."

"As you wish, sir," Maggie says.
Her voice is impatient now.
She wants him out of her kitchen, I can tell.
"I'll send William up with a tray very soon."

"Happy birthday, sir," I say.

"Johnny," he replies.

I risk a glance and he smiles.
"If anything arrives for me
will you send it straight up?"
I nod and Maggie wedges herself
between   us,
a rolling pin hanging by her side.
"Off you go now, sir, or you'll start to smell
as greasy as a scullery maid."

John Browning finally leaves—
        Johnny—
closing the door gently behind him.

"What in God's name was that all about?"
Maggie asks herself
and then me:
"What in God's name *was* that all about?"

But all I can focus on are William's words:
        The poor lad looks lost.

Like Other Men

Johnny spends the morning of his birthday
unloading a full cart
heavy with stone
       along with a handful of laborers and
stacking it against the wall
               farthest from the kitchen.

He doesn't work
as I imagine an aristocrat would,
daintily,
with an aversion to labor:
       he has energy,
       seems joyful.

He has his shirtsleeves rolled up
       and has to rest
         now and then.

He is not as strong or fast
as the other men,
       of course,
men who have spent their lives
                   in toil,
but Johnny is trying to keep up.

He *is* trying.

Then Again

He is taking a job
away from a local man,
              a laborer who needs the work,
a man like my father.

PART 3
Late September 1846

Decisions

The dregs of a long-gone summer sun scorches
the top of Daddy's head
as he scythes the last of the summer oats,
Owen and I following with pitchforks,
packing the grain into a cart.

Sweat, like teardrops,
runs down Daddy's face.
"That'll do for now," he says,
studying the bundles of grain
      ready for handing over to merchants
      headed to England.

"Wicken won't be patient
now he knows the potatoes are spoiled
and the oats are harvested.
He'll worry about payment."
Daddy traps a spider, watches it circle
      his palm in a panic.

"Maybe he'll wait until next year," Owen says.

"Wicken won't wait," I say instinctively,
without adding that the landlord
seems to have big plans for his estate.

Daddy releases the spider
gently into the field.
"We have to pay the rent
like we always do
or keep back the earnings and eat.
It's the workhouse or hunger.
That's the decision."
He sighs into the sky.

"Sooner or later we'll have to decide," he says.

Intervention

A commotion,
hollering and howling,
draws Maggie and me
from the kitchen
to the front of the house
where Silas Simmons,
Wicken's English valet,
is using a thick walking stick to beat a man
dressed in rags.

Each blow
causes the man to cry out,
his skinny frame curled up
into a ball by the front entrance
to the house.

"Comin' here and asking for charity
when Lord Wicken has
funded workhouses for you cretins."
Silas strikes the man again
and I can't help it—I let out a small scream.

Maggie pinches me.

Silas turns, and when he sees he is being watched,
lifts the walking stick once more.
I begin to move forward,
  to stop him,

but before I reach the pair
Johnny appears,
    pushing open the front doors
    and grabbing hold of the stick before
    it lands on the beggar.

Silas starts,
                bows his head very slightly.
"This tramp came to the door
scabbing for alms, sir.
I tried to make him leave quietly
but he's refused to go."

Johnny bends down to examine the man.
"Is he hurt?" he asks Silas.

Silas shrugs
    at the absurdness of the question,
then glances around at the small gathering:
kitchen staff and laborers,
    even the stable boy,
    who has run up the lane
    to watch.

But I cannot see Lord Wicken himself,
    neither outside
    nor at a window.
He must still be in Belfast.

Johnny speaks to the sprawled figure
on the ground.
"Can you move, sir?" he asks.

At this, Silas smirks,
and even I am surprised
to hear someone of Johnny's rank
address a beggar
with such regard.

The man moans.

Johnny returns the walking stick to Silas.
Then,
    with a movement of his hand,
    ushers the valet back inside.

Silas frowns. Stays right where he is.

Johnny turns my way but
addresses Maggie,
    who is standing next to me.
"Ask William to help me
move this man into the kitchen, Mrs. Kennedy.
And please fix him some broth."

Silas still hasn't moved.
It is like he is pasted to the spot,

glaring at the beggar, and at Johnny,
his face getting redder and redder.
"I was told—" he begins, outraged,
but Johnny raises his hand to silence him.
Then he puts two arms around the beggar
and hauls the man,
        who is mostly a sack of bones,
into a hunched, standing position.

Maggie grabs my arm. Come on now," she says,
                            and I go with her,
glancing back only once to see Silas
reluctantly shuffling inside
and Johnny holding up the beggar
and talking to him gently.

All This Happens

And still I don't mention
Johnny to anyone,
even when Mammy says,
"So what's the news from
The Big House today?"

By the River

"Hello," someone says,
       tapping my arm.

I start and swing,
not expecting anyone
to find me by the Rosserk River,
almost smacking Johnny's face
       with my book.

"I didn't mean to scare you," he says.
"I saw you wandering this way."

"I'm finished for the day, sir.
I just came to the river to get cool.
The kitchen can be steaming."

"I'm not checking up on you."
He eyes my book.
"You *really* like poems."

"I do."

"And you carry them everywhere with you."

"You don't even need to carry a book.
You can carry poems with you
if you memorize them, sir."

"And you do that?"

"Sometimes," I say,
then feel silly and boastful, having revealed my
learning.

But I don't want him to think I am a foolish girl,
that because I am a maid
I don't have a brain.

He sits on a rock
and watches the water wash over my feet.

I feel their nakedness.

"Have you time to go for a walk?" he asks.

"I have to get home," I say,
when really
no one would worry
if I got back a bit late.

"Of course.
I shouldn't have asked.
It's probably not a good idea anyway,
for us
to be seen gallivanting around together.
The trees have eyes."

"And wagging tongues, sir."

I use my skirt to dry off my feet
and begin to pull on my boots.

"My uncle talks a lot about the failed potato crop.
He says they are debating it in Westminster.
Have all the tenants been affected?"

"They have."

"Sounds serious."

"It's *very* serious," I explain.
"My brother says some children are too weak
to go to school.
The potatoes were the only hope
many people had of eating this winter."

"I didn't know this."

How can he be so naive?
Perhaps if you stay up at The Big House
every day and night
it's possible not to notice it.
"You saw that beggar for yourself.
People are starving already."

He considers this.
I stand up.
"Perhaps a walk another day?" he asks.
"If we went after dark and wore cloaks

no one would ever know who we were.
What do you say?"
He is joking.

     I know this.

So I say,
"I'm not sure it would be appropriate, sir."
It is not what I want to say.
I want to agree to a walk.
I want to agree to wearing cloaks in the nighttime.

     Something rustles in the bushes.

"I'm sorry, my parents will be expecting me back."

He watches me leave,
then stares into the river
as though he is
looking,
looking
     for something.

And as I race home
I stare into the sky,
wishing,
wishing
     for something

that I know
could never happen.

Daydreaming

For days I do not see
him in the yard with the laborers
nor by the outbuildings.

And when I go to the river
with a book
after work
        I am alone.

I do not see him around the grounds at all
as I scrub counters
and stare out the window
hoping to catch sight of him.

I do not hear his voice in the house
  or his footsteps.

Maggie says, "You're daydreaming."

I am.
It's true.

When I should be working.

When I should be worrying
how my family will survive
with only my meager wages.

I am daydreaming about a rich boy
with not a care in the world
who I am sure hardly thinks of me
         at all.

The Third Day

On the third day of his absence
Maggie says, "What's the sour face for?
You aren't paid to mope about."

"The rent is due," I say,
like she wouldn't know this already.

Maggie rolls her eyes.
"Well, that doesn't make you special."

So what would? I wonder.
What would make me special?

A Crust of Bread

Owen sits in the yard,
chewing on a thick crust of bread.

"What's that?" I ask.

"Someone came to the school
with bread and butter for all of us.
Master Sweeney said we could eat it in the
schoolroom or take it home."

"Was it a Quaker?" I ask.

"I don't know," he says.
"He was an English fella from The Big House.
He came yesterday too.
He had cake today but Master Sweeney said
    to give it to the girls."

"Cake?"

"Ellie O'Connell gave me a taste of hers.
She had to shave her head to get rid of lice.
        She didn't say it,
        but we all know."

"Be nice to Ellie. It isn't her fault," I warn him.

He gnaws the bread. "I know it isn't.
I told her she looked prettier that way."

"That was kind of you, Owen."

"It's true.
I'm going to marry Ellie O'Connell."

"Are you?"

"I am.
When I grow up I'm going to change my name
from Owen Quinn to Owen O'Connell and
live happily ever after."

"Are you?"

"I am." He offers me a piece of his bread.

"Do you know the boy from The Big House?"
he asks.

"I'm not sure," I say.

"You must know him!
I told him my name was Owen Quinn and he said
to tell my sister that walking is good for
your health.
Was he making a joke?"

"Maybe," I say.

Or maybe it was a message.

Commotion

Maggie has her ear pressed to the door
that separates the kitchen
from the rest of The Big House.
Every time I move she shushes me.
"Let me listen," she hisses.

I stand frozen,
and then I hear it myself:
banging and shouting.

I tiptoe across the stone floor
and ignore Maggie's scowl
when I press my ear to the door too.
"Do you think I am running a *charity*?"
Lord Wicken shouts.
"Did your mother send you here to spend
my money
or to help me make it?"

A voice responds
    but too faintly to be heard.

"If the children are hungry
and unable to go to get an education
then their parents should *feed* them!" he roars.
"And if they cannot do that, they should
take them to the workhouse.

That's why I pay my poor rates,
to provide for these people."

A pause and more soft talking.
"I did not put a roof over your head
so you could advise me of the misfortunes of
my tenants.
I know the problems well enough
and it is my pocket that pays for their relief
every time the bloody crops fail.
How much more should I give?
Should I sacrifice my whole fortune?
This estate and you and your sisters' futures?
First the beggar and now the children.
No more!"

A crash like something
falling to the floor.
"Do you hear me, John?"

Maggie steps away from the door
and blesses herself.
"Get back to the sink, girl," she says softly,
and just as I do, Lord Wicken
    bursts
into the kitchen.

I have never seen the landlord up
so close before:

                he is a giant.

A giant full of fury.

"Do not permit my nephew
to take anything from this kitchen
unless you have sought my approval," he hollers,
thumping his large fist against the table
    so violently it
    bounces off the floor.
"Not so much as a thimbleful of oil.
Do you understand, woman?"

"Yes, sir. I understand, sir."
Maggie seems to genuflect.

He notices me and exhales heavily.
"Who is *this*?"

"The new scullery maid, Lord Wicken.
Ellen Quinn.
She's proving herself to be a good worker, sir."

A good worker? Am I?
It's the first I've heard of it.

Wicken straightens his shoulders,
tries to compose himself.
"That applies to you too, wench.
Nothing to my nephew
until he proves he can be trusted."

I nod. "Very good, sir," I say.

And with that Lord Wicken
thunders from the kitchen.

Bruised

Johnny is trotting up the drove way
    on his horse.
I step aside to allow him to pass
but he slows to a stop.
"You owe me a walk," he says.
"I haven't forgotten."
He speaks
without any emotion at all,
without any joy.

"I told you, sir, it would be inappropriate."
I sound emotionless too.
But I am not.
I pity Johnny.
And somehow I pity myself.

On the side of his face is a ripening bruise—
given to him by Lord Wicken
    presumably.

"Could you please stop saying that?"

"Saying what, sir?"

"That. Saying *that*. Sir. *Sir, sir.*
I am *not* my uncle."
There is a sharpness in his tone,
something close to imperiousness.

"Then how should I address you,
Master Browning?"
I know I sound prickly.
I can't help it.
We are in dangerous territory
and I am the one more at risk.

"I've already told you," he says.

"You have, sir, yes."
I smile to show him I am not
    completely without feeling.
But it is not enough.

"Oh, forget it," he says,
and gallops away quickly.

In the Scullery

In the scullery,
by a mountain of dirty linens,
    is a small pile
    of poetry pamphlets
    along with a note.
"You might find these of interest.
    J."

I flick through the papers,
poetry by writers whose names
    I do not know.

My hands tingle
as I turn the pages,
scan the words,
inhale the rhymes
and melodies.

A gift.
Or a loan.
Stolen from Wicken's library, no doubt.

So we are both at risk now anyway.

Sunken

Rose's cheeks are slightly hollow.
I wonder what she is eating.
It can't be much.

In my pocket is a carrot
I've saved from dinner
and was going to give to Owen.
I offer it to her,
and with only a half-smile,
        a little ashamed,
she takes it.
"My parents won't be paying their rent," she says.
"If they do, they'll be dead of hunger by spring."
Rose runs her thumb over the ridges of the carrot.
Her skin is a little yellow in color.

"Are you well?" I ask.
We are sitting up on the hill
for the first time in weeks.
No bottle this time, no pipe or singing.

"Of course I am. I have this carrot, don't I?"
She laughs.
                It is as hollow as her cheeks.

"Is Eamon doing well?
I haven't seen him since the wedding."

"What'll happen
when they don't pay the rent?" she asks.

"I don't know," I say.

But it won't be good.

Peeling

I am in the yard peeling parsnips,
the dogs snuffling around me,
    no longer suspicious and snarly,
when Johnny appears around the corner.
He hesitates when he sees me,
looks about to walk backward,
then continues toward the door slowly.
"Miss Quinn," he says.

"Master Browning.
Thank you for the pamphlets.
I have them in the scullery
if you need them back."

"They won't be missed."

"Are you sure?
I wouldn't want your uncle to . . ."

Johnny waves away my worry.

And there is a long silence as
he tries to pull off his boots.
I continue with the peeling,
a bucket by my feet.

The bruise on his face is brown now,
but there are fresh bruises too,
purple dots along his forearm
as though someone has grabbed him roughly.

I reach toward him,
touch the little bruises.
"Does he do it a lot?" I ask.

"It's fine."

"No, it isn't fine," I say,
because it would be unfair to leave him feeling
friendless
in this place.

He looks down at my fingers.
"You're right. It isn't fine."

Making Plans

As I leave,
making my way
　　　down the boreen,
I spot Johnny by the stables
brushing a brown horse.

The stable boy is
mucking out straw.

They are sharing a joke.

Johnny sees me and calls,
runs to catch up.
"Nell! Wait!"

I turn.

"You've been reduced to
working in the stables," I say.

Johnny shrugs.
"If I don't keep busy, Uncle Dearest
will find much uglier diversions for me."

"If you ever fancy scrubbing sinks,
you're welcome to help me in the kitchen, *sir*," I say.

He shakes his head.
"No thank you, *miss,*
I think Mrs. Kennedy would beat me
to death with a whisk
if I tried to interfere in her domain."

"You aren't wrong," I say.

We laugh,
        and I like the sound of it,
        the feeling,
but when I glance up
at The Big House
I see through a wide window
the shadow of
          a figure
          watching us.

"Do you ride?" Johnny asks.
"We could go out one
evening, if you have free time.
Instead of a walk.
Since walks are deemed so improper."

I want to ask if he knows what it means
to be a person who isn't related to
      Lord Wicken.
The tenants don't own horses,

or houses.
We just about manage to feed ourselves,
and lately
some people can't even do that.

"I don't ride," I say.
And horse riding would be every bit as risky as
walking.
For him.
For me.

We shouldn't be arranging to do *anything*
when his uncle is demanding rents
from my neighbors
that none of them can afford,
when his uncle will arrive at our house
soon enough wanting his money,
when Johnny himself is to inherit this place,
        this land,
                this system.

"I'll teach you to ride," he says.
"If you teach me something in return?"

I think
        maybe
                he is flirting with me
but
before I can reply with something witty
a voice calls out.

"Master John. Master John, you're wanted
by Lord Wicken right away."
William Gaughan
is waving like a lunatic
        from the back door.

        The shadow at the window
        has gone.

"What does the old brute want now?"
Johnny mumbles.

"Perhaps he saw us speaking.
Can you imagine what he'd do if he saw
me perched on one of his precious steeds?"

"He wouldn't even know about it."

"Is it really worth the gamble?"

Johnny says nothing for a few moments,
thinking carefully about the question.
"I think so, yes," he says.

"Master John! Master John!"
The footman is making his way toward us.

"Give me peace," Johnny says.

"I have to get home," I say.

"Master John."
The footman is almost upon us.

> I turn away,
> dashing down the hill and
> smiling
> ever so
> slightly
> as I run.

What I Like

I like Johnny's eyes—
their darkness—
and how they stay on me
when I am talking,
how they do not   shift at all
to something else
as he listens.

I like the quietness of his voice,
which means I need
        to lean in
to hear him properly.

His kindness toward the schoolchildren.
The beggar.

His humor.

His hands.

The way his body moves as he works.

I like that Johnny is different from
everyone in the world I have met before.

And he seems to like me
a little bit.
        I like that too.

Daddy Would Raise Hell

But Daddy would raise hell
if he knew about Johnny.
I'm sure of it.

My whole life I have been
taught not to trust the British.
  "Bastards took our land,
    our language,
  would get rid of the lot of us too
  if they could," Daddy once said.

Still,
it is hard to resist
the offer of going riding.

And why should I?

Johnny showing up is the only
exciting thing to have happened
to me in sixteen years.

Why should my life be scrubbing floors,
worrying about hunger, and little else?

If Doctor Riley had known he was going to die
maybe he would have
done a few things differently.
I bet he would have gone
riding,
          if he'd had the chance.

We can't take risks from the grave.
It is too late by then.

Risk is what life is for.

In the Kitchen

I am dusting the shelves,
having removed every jar and bowl first,
setting things on the table,
when Johnny saunters into the kitchen.

Maggie half curtsies.
"Master John. Are you hungry?
If so, it would be better to speak with William or Silas
so you needn't
bother yourself coming in here.
It's awfully hot."

She is nervous,
I know, of Lord Wicken.
But she isn't wrong.
Steam hisses from every pot.
The fire is roiling,
                the walls sweating,
        even now it is cooler outside.

"I wanted to speak with Miss Quinn," he says.

Maggie bristles.

"Nell? Well now, I'm not sure
your uncle would approve of . . ."
She trails off,

realizing as she speaks
that she is implying something
        untoward
and is in no position to
make judgments about Johnny's behavior
or how he interacts with a maid.

I climb down from my stool
and tuck my duster into the band of my skirt.
"Master John," I say solemnly,
knowing Maggie is scrutinizing us,
that while she can't stand up to Johnny,
she could dismiss me in a second
and there's nothing anyone could do about it.

"Would you prefer to ride sidesaddle
or regular?" he asks.

"I already explained that I—"

Maggie quickly steps closer to us.
"Master John, if it's a riding companion
you need, I know Major Chambers
has two strapping sons.
And a niece, I believe."

"Thank you, Mrs. Kennedy.
Miss Quinn and I had plans to discuss literature

as well as ride.
I don't believe the Chambers
can recite their prayers with accuracy.
I doubt they have insight into
Shakespeare's sonnets."
He turns back to me.
"Miss Quinn?"
He is holding in a smirk,
and then so am I.

But I can feel Maggie's rising irritation,
        her anger that Johnny
        has noticed me at all.

Does he assume Maggie
won't tell Wicken about this?
If so, I think he is right:
only Silas has proven himself
to be a sneak
so far.

"I suppose regular would be fine," I whisper,
worrying that as a girl
I should have chosen
sidesaddle
                out of propriety,
immediately worrying that as a scullery maid
I should have said no to the whole plan.

"Good idea," he says. "Much safer."

"I didn't know it could be dangerous," I say.

"Please don't worry."

He bows before me
with a mocking solemnity
and I feel it:
a conspiracy
        between us,
and maybe something
truly dangerous.

I go back to the stool
to work at wiping the shelves.

"She's the scullery maid, Master John,"
Maggie snaps suddenly
        as Johnny is about to leave.

He turns.
"And you're the cook, Mrs. Kennedy," he says.
I assume he will tell her
that as the cook she would do well to
mind her own business
or risk his wrath.

But he does not.

He rests a hand on her shoulder instead
and says, "Thank you ever so much

for everything you do here.
Ignore my uncle's criticisms.
They are unfounded.
Your meals are delicious."

Punished

Maggie gives me much more
to do than usual,
scolding me
when I slow down,
questioning me constantly
about how well I know
Master Browning
and why we are riding
together.

It is the most fun day
I have ever had
in the kitchen.

Aching

I am aching from
scrubbing,
cleaning,
wiping.
And I know I'm needed at home
to help Daddy collect mushrooms
and Mammy make soup,
and that if they knew where I was
I'd be in hot water.

But when Johnny finds me
at the back door
wrapping myself in my shawl
ready to leave and says,
"My uncle's gone out for the evening.
    Shall we ride?"
I am unable to respond
in any other way:
    "I'd like that," I say.

Saddled Up

Johnny puts one palm over the other
to create a step
        so I can safely
                climb on to the
smooth gray horse he has already
saddled up.
"Her name's Willow and
she's as cool as Christmas morning," he says.
"But we'll go slowly at first. Take it easy."

He hands me the reins
and our hands briefly brush
    against one another.
"I'm terrified," I admit,
    surprised to feel so scared
    sitting up on a horse like this,
    imagining I'd have felt
    powerful.

"I'll be right next to you," he says,
jumping up on to his own brown filly.
"Agreed?"

"Agreed."

Slowly

We go very slowly,

our horses side by side,
our legs occasionally bumping
against one another.

And when I get the hang of walking,
Johnny shows me how to make Willow trot
and we do that together,
snaking our way along the lanes
as the mist rolls in from the ocean
and the darkness descends.

"Recite a poem for me," he says.

"I will not."

"We had a deal.
Horses in exchange for poetry."

"I'll recite a Shakespearean sonnet for you,
    if you like."

"What about something Irish?" he asks.

"You wouldn't understand it."

"I don't mind that."

"The English don't come off well," I say.

"I just want to hear your voice, Nell."

So I begin.
"Cois abhann Ghleanna an Chéama
in Uibh Laoire 'sea bhím-se . . ."
And Johnny is completely silent
    as I recite words my teacher taught me
    that I have held inside myself
    for so long,
        nowhere to put these sounds.

And afterwards, when I have finished,
I wonder how in hell
this has happened:
        that I have somehow connected
        with this English boy
        from The Big House
and am reciting Irish poetry to him.

Feelings

By the time we get back to the stables
    I am less afraid of the horse,

    but terrified of the
    feelings I am certain

    are growing stronger inside me.

His Hands

I have never wanted anyone's hands on me.

> But I think about Johnny's
> fingers around my waist,
> how he clutched me as
> I climbed down from the horse.

Even the thinking about it
> makes my body hum.

Strange

Mammy and Gilly are in our cottage blathering.
Rose and I are in the yard
sitting up on the stone wall.
It is Sunday morning
but no one goes to Mass anymore.

Rose plants her hands on her jutting hips.
"You seem not yourself," she says.

"Not like myself?"

"Strange, Nell. Not like yourself.
For a long time now."

"I don't know what you mean," I say.

This is not true.
I know I have gone quiet,
but I am afraid that if I speak
I will tell her
everything
and then
everything
will fall   apart.

"Has something bad happened?" she asks.
In her eyes there is real concern
and in my guts there is real guilt.

"I'm grand," I say.

A mouse scurries along the wall,

      slips into its crack,

then stays perfectly still,

         its tiny pink tail visible.

"I'm grand," I repeat. "Grand."

Collecting the Rent

It would make a whole heap
of sense to trade the oats
throughout the year
for bread or pieces of salty ham.

Still, when Wicken's bailiff comes to
the cottage to collect the rent,
pounding our door with his stick,
Daddy hands over every coin he has.
"We've nothing now," Daddy tells the bailiff,
whose waistline lets us know he
hasn't been affected by the blight.

"A lot of folks are suffering, Mr. Quinn," he says.
"Though it does seem like providence at times."

"What the hell is that meant to mean?"
Daddy and the bailiff are
        nose to nose.

"Men of good character
rarely allow their children to starve, Mr. Quinn."

"Winter is on the way. If people don't pay, then what?
We can't be thrown out like animals."

"Lord Wicken pays his poor rates," the bailiff says.
"And last year every landlord in Mayo raised
more than was required of him to feed the poor."

"Winter is almost upon us," Daddy repeats.

"Mr. Quinn, fecklessness cannot be rewarded
by charity.
It's up to people to save themselves.
And the worthy will survive.
Perhaps it's God's will."

"*Your* God's will.
Or your prime minister's. Your *queen's*."

"Be careful now, Mr. Quinn," the bailiff says
          very calmly.
He hauls himself up onto his horse
and gallops up the lane
toward the O'Connells' cottage.

Daddy punches a dent in the cottage wall
and cuts his knuckles.

"We'll be fine, Michael.
Haven't we got each other?"
Mammy says,
        as though love will be enough.

"And I have my job," I say.

Plus Johnny.
Who's on the inside.

PART 4
November 1846

An Announcement

Owen makes an announcement:
"Nell has a sweetheart."

"What? I do not."

"You do so.
Thomas O'Shea said he saw you
riding a horse with some fella.
Around and around yous went."
Owen makes kissing sounds
and I leap up to smack him.

Daddy wraps an arm around me.
"Take no notice of your brother."

"It isn't true, Daddy," I say.
            Technically I'm not lying.
            Johnny isn't my boyfriend.
            I have no idea what he is.

"I wouldn't be surprised if
the whole county was after you, Nell.
You get your looks from your father.
I don't think the Pope in Rome
could keep his eyes off you," Daddy says.

Mammy gives an exaggerated gasp.
"God forgive you," she says,
and goes back to her knitting.

In bed I shake Owen awake.
"Tell Thomas O'Shea that the next time
I see him he's in for it."

Owen groans.
"He said it definitely *was* you.
He said it was you and
that English lad from The Big House."

"I mean it, Owen.
Tell him to shut his trap.
And you better keep it bolted too,
if you know what's good for you.
No blabbing like you did
about Doctor Riley
when I told you not to."

Owen sits up.
"You do have a boyfriend," he says.
"You *do*, don't you, Nell?
I didn't believe Thomas.
He's always full of stories."

"Go to sleep," I say.
"And if Thomas starts up
his gossiping, you give him
a wallop from me."

Owen grins and nudges me
like we are plotting grand larceny.
"I'll hit him for you, Nell; don't you worry.
He'll not say another word."

Johnny's Story

Johnny finds me by the river again.
I have my boots on this time
so my skin is unexposed.
He holds out a handkerchief,
something carefully folded into its creases.
"It's a slice of lemon cake. If you'd like it.
I had to pinch it when
Mrs. Kennedy's back was turned."

"I'm not hungry," I lie. "You have it."

"I might," he says, sitting next to me.
He smells of peat and hot tea.
"I haven't seen you for a few days."

I thought of you every moment,
I want to admit. "I know," I say.
"Maggie has me half killed working."

"I kept thinking about the poem
you recited as we were out riding.
What was it about?"

"A battle. A land being fought over."

"I thought so. It's strange to be here
and know it isn't a place you're wanted."

I want you here, I think.

The birdsong in the trees around us
swells,
       is bewitching.

"Nell, can I ask . . .
Why are you working as a maid
when you have an education?"

"Because I'm poor," I admit, as gently as I can.
"We don't even work as maids usually.
My schoolteacher recommended me
on account of my learning.
It's as good as I'll ever get.
Girls whose parents are tenants on this land
don't go to finishing school."

He unwraps the cake and breaks it in two,
puts one half onto my lap
without asking and begins to eat
his piece.
I do the same.

It is sweet and bitter all at once,
filled with sugar and lemon juice.

"We're all trapped, I suppose," Johnny says.
"In different ways."

"What do you mean?"
I feel myself squint at this—
the stupidity of saying such a thing.
We may all be trapped
but not to the same degree.

He lowers his head.
"My uncle has no children
and I'm here to learn
how to manage the estate.
He won't leave the running of things
to an agent
                    and insists I shouldn't either."

"You're his heir?" I ask, though I know the answer.

He nods. "All going well.
I was taken out of school and brought here
by my brother-in-law, like I said.
It was the first time I'd ever met my uncle.
Have you had that privilege?"

I nod. Say nothing.

"He's menacing.
As soon as I arrived he threw
away my paints and told me

I needed to learn to be a man.

'Artists are not men,' he said.

Try telling that to Turner.

But it was meant to be my older brother here.

Charlie. He was the original heir."

"Why isn't he here?

Why were you sent?"

"Charlie died. In a bar brawl of all things.

We aren't meant to talk about it.

But he didn't want to come here.

He'd fallen in love with an Italian girl

and planned to move to Tuscany."

"I'm sorry about your brother."

He hangs his head.

"He was a good person.

He was an awful drunk, but he was my best friend.

My father died when I was ten.

My mother never remarried.

She's hung all her hopes on this place,

and without my brother

she's hung all her hopes on me.

I have five sisters.

Without this estate we'll all be penniless.

I don't have to tell *you* how it is for women."

"Will they move here?" I ask.

"There's more chance of my uncle
taking up ballet and moving to Paris."
He laughs.
And the sound is so beautiful
against all the pain and
complications he has described.

"You're by yourself here," I say.

He nudges me. "Not anymore."
He pops a little more cake into his mouth.
"Now I have you."

New Baby

Maggie wraps her shawl around her shoulders.
"I'm warning you," she says.
"If I get back here and the dinner's spoiled
because you let the pies dry out
or the bread burn,
I'll take a poker to your shins."

Her youngest, Eileen, has given birth,
but the baby boy is struggling.

"He's blue," says Joe, Maggie's son-in-law,
who stands just inside the door,
a look of fear smeared across his bony face.
"He can breathe grand, but the color
won't change on him."

"Gilly might be the best one to help," I say.

Maggie nods begrudgingly and turns to Joe.
"Run down to the McElligotts by the
crossroads and tell Gilly to come.
Get a move on, Joseph."

Joe gets going.

He's no more than eighteen,
    I'd say,
and has the worry of being a father
    already.

Outside, the wind bends
     the trees sideways.
Rain falls
       horizontally.

"You can use my shawl for your head," I say.

Maggie blinks but cannot be gracious.
"Keep your eyes on those lamb pies
and check the meat every half an hour."

The Helper

Johnny pops his head into the kitchen.
"I saw the old crone go out," he whispers,
though there is no one else around.

I place a lid back onto a pot of cabbage.
"She's had an emergency," I say,
removing my white cap
and stuffing it into the pocket of my skirt
so I look less like a servant.

He comes in and closes the door.
"Good morning, Nell."
He smiles, using every feature in his face.

"Good morning, sir," I reply.

He grins. "How long will Hecate be gone?"

"No idea. A while."

His grin widens.
He grabs my hand. "Come with me."

I pull away.

"I can't. I'm in charge of the dinner."
I wave my arms around
at all the steam and smells.

"And anyway, what about your uncle?
Be sensible, Johnny."

"My uncle's gone to Killala
        to meet a magistrate there on some business.
        He's out until this afternoon.
        I want to show you around."

"Are you deranged?
        Do you know what would happen
        if I was caught?"

He laughs. "You won't be caught."

"Even if I wasn't, I told you—
        I have to make the dinner."

"Would it be quicker if I helped?"

"You *are* deranged."

"Show me what to do," he says.

A Recipe for Forgetting

Johnny	chops
and	stirs
and	sieves
and	checks
and	tastes
and	cleans
and	scrubs
and	all the while
he	is smiling
as	I sing
or	recite poems
and	making me laugh
at	his silly mistakes
so	I forget
for	a while
what's	
outside	this house—
the	hunger
and	loss
	everywhere,
the	unfairness
in	everything,
my	fears
for	our future.
I	forget
we are together
here	only

in this

      moment

and   could

      never

      ever

be   like this

beyond   today.

Once We Are Finished

Johnny sneaks me into the library.
It is painted in deep reds
with tapestries and oil paintings on every wall.
It smells of soot and spices.
Johnny pours two large measures of
Wicken's whiskey from a decanter.
I drink it down in one go.
It sears my throat.

On the wall is the hairy head of a boar
with long tusks.
It is out of place
beside the stiff portraits
framed in gold
of important men
in military uniforms.
The dead boar is grisly.
Johnny says, "He killed that one himself."

"I see."

"My uncle spent some time in India,
and while he was there he hunted boar
from horseback
with spears."

"What for?" I ask.

"For fun," he says flatly.
The fire is roaring,
      has clearly been tended to,
      and I worry that William
      or Silas
or one of the other servants
will slink into the library and see us.

Johnny senses my unease.
"Let's go upstairs," he says.

I hesitate.
But for less than one tick
on the grandfather clock
standing guard
in the corner.

A Fire Burns

A fire burns
            in the corner of Johnny's bedroom
too.

And from his window
is a view of the whole
village rolling right
down to the
squally sea.

The furniture is ornate,
     polished,
gleaming like nothing
I have ever known before.

"I've seen pictures in books," I say,
"of English houses. It's like a fairy tale."

On the floor next to the fire
are piles of paper with sketches on them
and a jar containing pencils
and chunks of charcoal.

I kneel. "What's all this?"

"Just some drawings. Nothing much."

Johnny has sketched
        pictures of the landscape,
                the stables,
        the sea,
        portraits of people
        and
        among them
        me:
                a gaunt girl
        with messy hair,
        an upturned nose
        and large eyes.

"They're roughs," he says,
snatching the sketches from me
self-consciously.
"If you sat for me, I could do a better job of it."
He shuffles through the papers.
"This is my brother, Charlie," he says.
It is a small drawing of a young man
        reading in an armchair,
                a dog at his feet.
"It's the only picture I drew of him."

"It's perfect," I say.

"And this is my sister Helena."
He shows me another drawing,
        of a young woman
standing by a fireplace,

holding up her silky skirts to warm
her bottom.

"She hated it when I showed her.
Told me it made her look unrefined."

"I'm not surprised!"

"But it's so her.
She's always cold.
If you can't find Helena,
find a fire and she'll be close by.
And she isn't refined.
She makes my mother choke
with the things she says."

"You miss her?"

"If I don't make things work here in Mayo
she'll have to marry some dimwit with a fortune.
She doesn't want to do that."

"Would she rather marry a dimwit with no fortune?"

Johnny laughs, opens a drawer in a dresser.
"Since my uncle banned me from painting
I've started to whittle," he says,
showing me a wood carving
of what I think will become a figurine.
        The marks are rough.

It is unfinished.

"That's why I was sketching you," he says.
"But it's hard from memory."

"You're making me into a statuette?"

"No. Yes. Is that alarming?"
He is uneasy now,
fiddling with the wood carving
between his fingers.

I stand, run my hand along
        the embroidered edges of
        the blankets on his bed.
"Not alarming, no," I say.
"It's astonishing."

In the Hallway

Before I manage to steal
back into the kitchen
I bump into
Silas Simmons
as he leaves the library
with a small tray.
He nods at me,
then looks up the stairs
to where Johnny is
standing with his hand
on the railing.
"Sir," is all Silas says.

But he is smirking.

It is not a good sign.

A Surprise

Rose and Eamon have fallen out.
"I've had enough of him," she says.

We are walking along the river,
picking berries as we go.
They are mostly gone now,
withered away with the cold.

"He's your husband.
You can't get rid of him."

Rose snorts. "I could murder him,
which is what I'm close to doing.
He told me last night he thinks
Caroline Kelly has a fine pair of legs on her.
She's about forty."

I can't help being pleased.
Even though they're married,
Rose and Eamon haven't changed—
still sniping, sparring.

"How's Maggie treating you?" she asks.
"We hardly see you these days."

"Maggie Kennedy is more bark than bite.
But she watches me like a raven."

A rabbit darts between the trees.
       Rose lets out a scream
       then reaches toward a berry
              to pick it.

I consider finally
confiding in her about Johnny,
       the horse riding,
       the feelings keeping me awake at night.

But then she says,
"What's Wicken's successor like?
Have you seen him at The Big House?"

"Why?"

"I wondered, is all.
Eamon and his brothers were planning
on surprising
the British brat
when he goes out shooting or whatever
those imbeciles do for fun."

"Surprising him how?" I ask.
I keep my tone steady
though I am petrified
                     the Flynns
have already done something
awful to Johnny.

And he doesn't deserve it.
He hasn't laid a finger on anyone.
If anything, he's been trying to help.

"They just want him to know the boys here
won't be pushed around.
He's young, they say. Our age.
The face of a cherub, by all accounts.
An English cherub." She snorts. "Not likely."

"Eamon needs to be careful.
Wicken will set soldiers after him
if his nephew is attacked.
He can be brutal."

Rose shrugs.
"They were just going to scare him."

"Tell them not to."

Rose stops walking.
"What's going on, Nell?
Something's changed since
you started working up there."

"Nothing," I lie. "I just don't want Eamon to
    come to any harm."

Or Johnny.
I don't want him to come
to any harm either.

The Baby Is Better

Maggie's grandchild has recovered,
is a normal color now,
thanks to Gilly McElligott.
And Maggie is easier on me,
talks a lot more
and not just to snarl at me:

"Gilly McElligott might be a mouth,
but she's got a knack when it comes to healing.
One look at that baby and she knew what it needed.
I'd have been lost, I don't mind admitting it.
And she didn't ask for a thing.
I gave her a turnip. I'm not mean.
But she didn't ask,
and I could see by the rags she was in
she could have done with help.
My Eileen was in an awful state.
And wasn't I relieved to get back here
and see you'd kept at your chores
and didn't spend the time God gave you for work
daydreaming like some of the mindless girls
I've had around the place over the years.
I was ready to give you a clobber.
I was sure you'd be up to no good.
Get on with those vegetables now;
stop gawking at me like you can't listen
and work at the same time.
What's wrong with you?

I want them sliced and boiled.
And don't skimp on the salt."

Road Works

The government is paying
a few pennies per day to anyone
willing to do hard labor
on the roads.
So Daddy, Bobby McElligott, and Eamon,
along with a few other men,
go to see what they can get.

Gilly McElligott tells Mammy
you have to be destitute to get anything.
That even the workhouses
are turning people away.

"What does *destitute* mean?" Mammy says,
looking at Owen
huddled in the corner like a
premature pup waiting on
the milk Mammy's heating up for him.

"You have to be living in a bog hole," Rose says.
"But the rest of us hardly live in Bunratty Castle."

"What's it like in The Big House?" Gilly asks.

"What do you mean?"
        I feel my face redden.

Rose notices, tilts her head.

"Is there plenty to eat?
The cook has enough coming in
to feed everyone, does she?" Gilly asks.

"More than enough," I say,
thinking of Wicken's slobbering dogs
licking up meat from the floor.

"It isn't right," Mammy says.

"It isn't right," Gilly agrees.

And I know it's true.
It isn't right.

Rejected

"They wouldn't take us
for the road works," Daddy says.
They have enough men. And even if they hadn't
we couldn't survive on what they're offering.
But you know some of the roads they're building
don't go anywhere?"

"I don't understand," I say.

"The roads just peter out.
       They lead to bogs or cliff edges.
              They go nowhere."
Daddy stacks turf,
making a meal of it.
       His muscles are all gone.
"Another great idea from those across the sea.
Tell me how they can know
what's best for our people."

"Has something happened in England?" I ask.
I pile the turf against the wall,
to give him time to wipe his forehead.
The palms of his hands are red raw.

"Gobshites, all of them,
debating our lives
in the same way they'd argue over
what to wear for dinner."

He hitches up his loose trousers,
       spits nothing into the ground.

I think of Johnny,
wonder whether he has to dress for dinner
to please his uncle.

"Has Wicken paid you for last week yet?"
Daddy asks.

"It's due tomorrow.
How long have we left before things get bad?"

My father doesn't ask me to clarify the question.
"Don't worry, Nell.
I'll think of something."
He pulls me into his arms.
"I won't be long thinking of something,
and when I do, I'll ask for your help, I promise."

Target

Johnny waits for me
      at the crossroads after work,
way beyond the gates of The Big House
so Wicken won't see us together.

It is rare for Johnny to leave The Big House,
nothing for him beyond its boundary.

We talk about his sister and my brother,
and art and poetry,
treading carefully—
a mist this evening
making it difficult to see
much farther than a few steps ahead.

Then I say,
"You should be careful when you're out.
Especially if you're alone."

"What do you mean?" he asks.

He must have heard about the mishaps
that have befallen landlords
in neighboring counties,
the attacks on the rich.
Surely I don't need to spell it out,
and I can't betray Eamon.

"I mean be careful.
Some people are desperate.
And angry."

"Angry," he repeats, chewing over the word.
"Yes, I suppose they would be."

Gertie

The goat is spindly-legged and milkless.
      Her eyes
      bulge in their watery sockets.

Daddy can no longer watch her
grind her teeth on weeds
so takes a blade
and cleanly
cuts the goat's throat,
      blood spraying against
      his face, trousers, the trees,
      seeping into the gravel
      like red rain.

After grace we eat silently,
tender goat cooked over an outside fire,
our fingers powdered in charcoal
from the burnt flesh.

When we are done
Daddy takes half the remaining meat
to our neighbors in exchange for
whatever they can offer,
trades with them,
even if that trade means
goat for them and nothing at all for us.

Because this is the stuff my father is made of.

Owen Whimpers

Owen whimpers all night long.

He loved Gertie.
"She's in heaven now with the angels," I tell him.

"She is in her hole," he says.

Sling

"Master John!" Maggie cries.

Johnny's arm is in a sling.
He sits at the kitchen table
and she brings him some water.

"What happened?" I ask.

"I fell off my horse," he says,
sipping from the glass.
"She got spooked by something
and reared up.
Knocked me onto my back."

"Where were you?
I told you to be careful," I say.

Maggie blesses herself.
"You *should* be careful, sir.
Thank God you didn't
break your neck."

"She's so steady,
it makes no sense," he says.

But it does to me:
                Eamon.

Peace and Quiet

His arm is still in a sling.
We do not talk about it.

"Tell me more about your sister," I say.

"Helena?"
Johnny uses a thumb to smooth away clay
from a blue pebble and throws
it into the rising river.
"She's crazy for birds. And swimming.
Even in the winter. She isn't afraid of ice."
  He finds another pebble
    and hurls it hard into the
      trickling water next to us.

"And do you take after her at all?
Helena?"

"I like swimming too,
but I'd have to take off my clothes.
That would be the sensible thing.
And the frightening thing!"

"I'd look away. I promise."

He smiles and lowers his eyes.
"Helena would like you.
She reads a lot too.
And doesn't like convention.
My brother, Charlie, would have been too
      drunk to notice you."

Johnny edges closer, rests his head on my shoulder.
I inhale deeply and hold my breath—
      cannot find the strength to exhale.
"Father, I'm not so sure.
He'd probably not have said either way.
My father liked being left alone
with his newspaper," he says.

"I wish you hadn't lost them," I say finally.

"Me too," he says.
"But then I wouldn't have found you."

Traitor

"They scared the horse
and he fell off and hurt his finger
or his arm or something.
Why do you care about
some jumped-up English dolt?"
I am at Rose's place on the pretense
of collecting some mint for my mother.

"He could have smashed open his skull," I say.
"They could have killed him."

"It's as much as he deserves.
They're already evicting people, Nell.
Did you know that?
The bailiff told my da he has
to pay,
and quickly,
or the lot of us are out.
In this cold? It's barbaric."

"But the nephew isn't responsible.
He's seventeen years old."

Slowly
    Rose ties the mint with some string,
    hands it to me.
"You're sweet on him."

"Oh, give over, Rose."
I stuff the mint into the pocket of my skirt,
    tie my headscarf tighter.

"Look around you at what's happening, Nell.
The whole country is sinking
and the likes of Lord Wicken
are making it worse.
You've been in that house and seen all he has.
Couldn't he let us keep the money from the oats
just until the potatoes right themselves?
Wise up, Nell.
You might work there now
but they think you're no better
than the lambs they slaughter for their supper."

"That isn't true. Johnny isn't that way."

"Johnny? Johnny?
Oh, Nell, don't tell me you're
involved with him."

She steps toward me,
tucks lose strands of hair behind my ears.
"Please tell me you aren't in love."

"Ask Eamon not to hurt him."

"Ask Eamon yourself."

I spin around.
Eamon is standing in the doorway.
"Traitor."

That is all he says.

What Have I Done?

Johnny and I talk.

He's English but not
     All Bad
and now I'm some sort of
traitor?

It makes no sense.

None.

Waiting

Silas Simmons is smoking a pipe.

He has been there a while;
I can tell by his bitter look
as I fill the coal scuttle,
shoveling from the pile in the shed.

"Miss Quinn," he says slyly.
"How are ya, my dear?"

"Mr. Simmons."
        I do not meet his gaze.
He has not waited by the shed
to exchange pleasantries
or pick up coal for the house.

He wants something.
        And I'm not naive enough
        to have to wonder what it is.

"I'm impressed that
you've caught Master John's eye.
But you'd best be careful with these blue bloods.
He'll use you up and chuck you out.

And if Lord Wicken
        were to discover it, well . . ."

He puffs on the pipe.

"I have no idea what you mean, Mr. Simmons.
Master John needed a tray taken to him."

"Yeah.
Cos there ain't a valet for that."

"You couldn't be found.
Nor could William."

"You've got all the answers."

Silas is not standing close to me,
        and then
        he is,
        my chin pinched between
        his fingers,
        his sour breath against my face.
"*I* need some help now," he sneers
    through brown teeth.

I push him away,
        ready to kick and spit if I have to,
        when Maggie appears around the corner.

She sees us
        and starts,

looks first at Silas and then at me.
       She straightens up.
"Mr. Simmons, could you be a gentleman
and carry that coal scuttle into the kitchen for us?
It looks terrible heavy."

       Silas is silent.
       He lifts the scuttle and
       carefully steps away.

Maggie hands me a pile of wet rags.
       "*You*, hang these on the line."
And in a lower voice,
       "Keep away from him.
       Whatever you do, don't let yourself
       be caught with Silas Simmons.
       You hear me, girl?
       Get on now, hang up those rags."

       "Thank you, Mrs. Kennedy."

Friends

Johnny was to walk me
      to the crossroads
but the heavy rain is back.

We take shelter in the stables,
brush the horses with
long strokes
that make the animals purr like kittens.

"You're not to do *anything*," I tell him
when Johnny threatens
to use a poker on Silas Simmons
the next time he sees him.

"He practically attacked you, Nell."

"He didn't hurt me. I'm fine.
If you do anything,
he'll snitch and you'll be in for it."

The sun has set.
      He lights a candle.

"Why would *I* be in trouble?" he asks.

"For inviting me upstairs.
I'm not your equal."

He winces. "Why are you saying that?"
He looks sad,
        like I've tried to hurt him
when I am trying to speak the truth.
A truth he knows.

It doesn't matter how many books I read
or the number of sonnets I can recite.
It doesn't matter that I was top in my class
and that Owen's as smart as I am.
        I could be a genius
and I'd still be a scullery maid
and one of Wicken's tenants.

Johnny
        on the other hand
will be rich
        and he doesn't have to
        fight for it.
Not like everyone else has to.

"Your uncle would be indignant
if he knew we were close.
He's already irate.
You have to keep me hidden from him
like I keep you hidden from my family."

"You *hide* me?"

"You're the enemy, Johnny.

You must know that.
To people around here
you represent something terrible.
You think your horse bucking was an accident?"

"What do you mean?"

"Nothing."

"Nell?"

"I can't say any more, Johnny.
But you have to be vigilant.
And so do I."

"I don't want to be heir to this place," he says,
his anger rising.

"But you are. And in ten or twenty years you'll
own all of this. You'll own everyone."

"I don't want to *own* people, Nell.
What are you trying to say?"

"I'm saying keep away from Silas
or he'll retaliate and tell your uncle.
Then I'll lose my job
and my family will have less than nothing."

He takes the grooming brush from me

and then he takes my hand, holds it.

And we stand
     in the candlelight
    hand in hand,
    side by side,
    still and silent,
    neither of us alone.

"When I'm with you, I feel like a person," he says.

By Candlelight

Wind wails.

The sky booms and cracks.

But I am not afraid of the weather,
      the lightning,
      the thunder.

I am not even afraid of being found out.

I am in Johnny's arms
and his mouth is on my mouth.

I pull him toward me,
        we kiss and
           clutch,
and though I have spent
my life believing in God,
it is the first time
I know He is real
and good
because pleasure
like this
exists
and I am alive on this earth
to feel it.

Back Home

I lie awake
for hours,
remembering,
replaying,
reliving
every second
of my time with Johnny.

I hardly sleep
at all.

The Morning After

Lord Wicken smokes a stocky cigar.
I inhale its sweetness.
Johnny is standing next to his chair.
He is looking at the rug.

The fire fizzles in the grate.

Wicken clears his nose through his mouth,
swallows whatever has come up.
"Allegedly you have been creeping
around my house like a little mouse," he says
very leisurely.

But he is stifling something.

"Excuse me, Lord Wicken?"

"*Allegedly,* though I cannot for one second
imagine it's true,
you were upstairs in this house
and seen talking to my nephew."

Johnny looks up at last,
    gives me a pleading look.

But how am I to interpret it?
What does he want me to say?
And why doesn't he speak
when he sees me hesitate?

"Lord Wicken, I'm sorry if I
offended you at all.
William was otherwise engaged.
I was simply delivering
a tray to Master Browning, I . . ."

Lord Wicken raises a hand to make me stop.
"Lucky for you, John has told me the same story.
So

    perhaps it's true."

"It's true, sir," I say.

Wicken drums his fingers against the armrests.
"My valet does have a history
of being somewhat zealous in his fears,
especially when he has set his eye on something.
He has what I'd call a weakness.
And yet . . ."
He examines me

       up and down
       as though I am livestock
       at a market and he is wondering
       about my price.
"Do not ever deem yourself equal to us.
Any kind of fraternizing
with this family
and you will be out on your ear.
Do you hear?"

I bow,
        am ready to scrape myself
        against the floorboards to please him
and escape.

Johnny remains silent.
Wicken looks up at his nephew.
"She's not bad looking, is she?"

"I hadn't noticed, sir," he says.

Wicken puffs again on his cigar,
seems bored all of a sudden.
"Right. Out of my sight," he tells me.
"And never come into this
part of the house again.
Stay in the kitchen where you belong."

PART 5
December 1846

A Present

Johnny pulls a parcel of paper from his pocket.

"A Christmas present," he says.
We are in the stables.
It is so cold I have to hide
my hands in my armpits
to keep them warm.
I can see my own breath between us.
>   And his.

"I don't have anything for you," I say.
We have not spoken in a week,
merely exchanged terrified glances.
>   He is scared
>   and so am I.
Of what would happen
if we were caught
being more than master and servant
toward each other.

I take the gift, open it up.
A small wooden carving—
>   a girl.
No.
>   He has whittled
>   a woman.

My body flutters.

I run my finger over the figure,
feeling all the places he carved,
the body parts he had to
imagine when he made it.

I tuck my chin into my chest
to hide my face.

"I think about you every minute.
I hate how overpowering it feels," he says.

I nod. Because I understand.
I am the same way
and every noise in The Big House
makes me wonder about him.

Johnny nudges me.
"The carving has a teeny-tiny
          gray stone in the body.
A stone where the heart should be."

I squint and look closer,
          see no stone
          and smile.
"I'm a very warm person.
That's not funny."

"It is a little bit," he says.

Beautiful

The wood carving is beautiful.

And I can hardly believe that
it doesn't matter
if my hair is seaweed,
my pockets are torn,
my ribs stick out,
or I get flaming spots
on the tip of my nose.

Johnny sees something in me
worth committing to permanence.

And Yet

And yet
what Johnny doesn't know

is that although I adore
    the carving,
    my family is now
    close to starving
    and even better than a
    piece of dead wood
    would have been
    a dead chicken.

Silent

"What's *wrong* with you?" Mammy says.

"Huh?"

"You're in your own world."
We are eating bowls of broth
with little bits of salmon floating in it,
a treat from Maggie for Christmas
after we'd made the dinner
for Wicken and his guests.

"She's fretting about all
the dishes she'll have to wash
tomorrow, aren't you, Nell?"
　　Owen says, and elbows me.

"You haven't said a word
all evening. Are you sick?" Daddy asks.

"I don't think so," I say.

Still.

I don't feel like myself.

Princely

I drop the wooden carving
and it rolls along the floor,
making a complete spectacle of itself.

Daddy scoops it up,
feels it between his bony fingers.
"What's this?"

My face is fire.
"Stop it, Daddy. It's nothing," I say.

He hands it back. "Looks like something to me.
Looks like something very *very* to me.
So tell us, why was Bobby McElligott
asking about our plans for you last week?
Is Patrick courting you?"

"Pat McElligott?
He's thirteen, Daddy.
It isn't from him," is all I manage.

"Well, whoever it's from should talk to me first, Nell,
before he starts any sort of carry-on.
And if I'm to approve, he'll need to fill up your guts.
Does he do that?"

"Daddy, please stop, it's nothing."

"It's from me," Owen says,
reaching for the carving to see it.
Shyly I hold open my palm to show him.

"It's so dainty," Mammy says.
"Did you really make that, Owen?"

My brother proudly says
he did, and starts to explain
exactly how he whittled it.

"Your father stole a scone
for me once," Mammy says,
once Owen has finished lying
his arse off.
"Gave me flowers in the spring.
Blackberries in the autumn.
We used to talk until our throats were tender.
Do you remember those days, Michael?"

"What do you mean, *do I remember*?
Right. Get up, Mary!" Daddy demands.
"We're going out."

He holds Mammy's hands and kisses them.
Then he kisses her cheeks. Her neck.
"Michael, will you mind yourself!"
Mammy tries swatting him away.

"Look after your brother, Nell.
I have romancing to attend to," Daddy says,
and drags Mammy from the cottage.

"Where are they going in the dark?" Owen asks.
"What if the fairies find them?
Or they could fall in a ditch.
Or meet a bad fairy."

"They want to be alone," I tell him,
            like this is obvious,
            and put the carving back
            into my pocket.

"What's the name of your fella?" Owen asks.
"Is it John Browning?"

 "I don't have a fella."

"Well, what's the name of the fella
who made that little yoke?"

"Johnny," I confess.
"You aren't to tell anyone, do you hear me?
He does live up in The Big House."

"Is he a prince?"

"I don't think so."

"Is he nice?"

"He's very nice."

Owen lies back on the bed,
his hands under his head.
"If you marry him,
would *I* become a prince?" he asks.

"You're already a prince," I tell him.

Thinking

"Where are you rushing off to
at daybreak?" Daddy asks,
catching me in the yard.

"I've to get to The Big House early," I say.
"Maggie needs me to light the stove.
And we've a huge clear-up after yesterday."

My father isn't soft, but he lets me
leave without an interrogation.

By the crossroads, Johnny is waiting.
When he sees me he jumps up,
jogs over, and kisses me.
"I thought of you all night."
He smiles.

I hit him.

"Didn't you think of me?"

"I did," I say.

Love Sick

I feel sick
    all
    the
    time.

My stomach churns, turns, and tips,
not just when I see Johnny,
but when I think of him—
and even when I don't.

The feeling is fiercest when we meet
to share stories and hold hands,
tucked into a corner of the stables.

Kissing makes the sickness worse:
the yearning,
the burning in my belly,
the slow learning of each other.

Even if there were plenty of potatoes
in our house, I couldn't eat

               a
               single
               one
without being nauseous.

I think they call it   love.

Johnny and Owen

They are by the well,
sitting together
like old friends,
Owen with a piece of wood
in his hand,
Johnny showing him
how to carve into it with a small knife.
"Nell!" Owen shouts.
"Turns out the English
aren't all bad!"

"Hello, Miss Quinn," Johnny says,
and winks.

"Master Browning."

Owen rolls his eyes.
"I know you two are going together.
You don't have to hide it."

I lower the bucket into the well,
my back to them,
unable to keep from grinning.

Because it does feel nice—
not to be in hiding
for once,
not to have to keep Johnny
a secret.

Maybe it was the secret
and not love
that was making me sick.

Last Rites

Johnny and I are walking, talking,
snorting about the way Owen
is learning his prayers to impress the priest.
"He told me he'd like to be a priest,
that he's not a huge fan of girls anyway," Johnny says.

"The cheek! He's living with two women!"

Johnny laughs. "I'm sure he'd be no better
in a monastery than I would."

"I think you'd cope," I tease,
brushing his arm with my fingertips.

Johnny pulls me close,
nuzzles his face against my neck,
and barks.
I scream,
laughing.
We are loud.
Almost obscene.

But
we stop short.

A man is barring our way,
sprawled on the road before us.
His eyes are only half open.

"Is he dead?"
Johnny takes a step forward
and then a second step back.
"You shouldn't touch him.
He could be diseased."

"We can't just leave him there," I say.

      The man groans.
      His fingers twitch.

I approach slowly.
The man's breath is quick, shallow.
He smells of piss and vomit.
"He needs milk. Or water at least."
I push back the man's hair from his face.

He opens his bulgy eyes.
"Last rites," he says slowly.

I lift his head on to my lap.
"Find him something!" I shout at Johnny,
ignoring the man's request for a priest.
"Please."

Johnny stays where he is;
his hands hang by his side.
"He can't be helped," he says quietly.
And he starts to pray.
"' Our Father, who art in heaven . . .'"

"What are you doing?
He's dying. He'll die."

Johnny sticks with mumbling prayers.

The man wheezes.
His breath comes more slowly.

And then he quietly closes his eyes,
opens his mouth,
                        and dies.

Midwinter

The winter thickens:
fields are hard as rock
and white with rime.

Slowly
our neighbors
begin to leave.
There is talk of evictions
and no one wants to
wait for that.

Some go to America,
some to the workhouses,
although William says
they're full now
and taking no one.

It is a little like living in hell,
if hell were all ice and not hot
as the Bible tells us.

Together

"I made another one," Johnny says.
He holds out a new carving. "It's me.
I thought you should have him too.
I thought they should be together."

I run my hand along the figurine
and my body shudders,
thinking about how it feels
to touch the real Johnny.

"What's happening to the land?" I ask.
"There's talk of evictions."

Johnny scratches his head,
seems confused. But he must know.
"I think my uncle intends to use the fields for cattle.
Cattle are profitable."

"And how will he clear the land?"

"Your father paid him. You told me that."

"But hardly anyone else paid.
What will happen to them?
What will happen to this village,
        to my friends?"

"Oh, God, Nell.
I really don't know," he says.

The Shore

"Let's go to the shore.
See what there is," Daddy says,
his voice full of color,
like we might detect a pirate ship
                         on a distant wave
or spot a mermaid
                  swimming in the shallows.

But he's off to find food—
scavenge for our dinner.
It is two days until I get paid
and there is nothing at home to eat.
Daddy hums to make light of it,
throws a blanket into a basket
and the whole burden
over his shoulder.

I put on my boots.
Owen does the same.

By the shore,
droves of ordinary people are
grubbing for weeds and urchins in the rocks,
children so hungry
they chew on whatever they discover
without waiting to take it home to cook,
          certainly not bothering to say grace
          before gobbling it down.

Daddy tells me to use the blanket for gathering.
"Seaweed will do," he says.
"Unless you find a pheasant!"

He wades into heavy ocean waves
        looking for fish.

"Is that Christina?" Owen mutters,
nodding at a child,
unmistakably one of Sissy Doyle's girls.

"It is," I say.
        Christina's legs are bird-thin,
        bruised.
            She is by herself
        but can be no older than
        six or seven years old.
Owen takes a handful of seaweed
over to her and she starts to eat it.

He sits with her then,
and the two of them begin to smile.

When Daddy steps out of the sea
he is drenched,
                empty-handed.
"You'd need a strong net to catch
anything in that," he says.

So we head home with nothing except
a stack of salty seaweed in the basket,
and the shame of knowing
we're no better than anyone else.

Keening

Heavy with damp and backache,
we come across a woman keening,
kneeling next to a cottage with no roof.
        Her cheeks are hollow.
        Her clothes are clotted with mud.
"What's your trouble?" Daddy asks,
crouching next to her.
"They took the roof," she says.
"They took the roof and they took my husband."

"What did he do?" Daddy asks.

The woman beats her breast,
keens some more into the fog.
I step back slightly, hold Owen's hand.
"He found a sheep in the field beyond.
We weren't to know it belonged to Wicken.
How were we to know?"

Daddy sets down the basket,
fills his hands with seaweed,
lays it next to the woman.
"You can cook this," he says.
"Try to get something into you
before the day is out.
Weeping won't bring back your man."

"He'll be hanged," she says.

"He'll do hard labor," Daddy corrects her.
"Just keep yourself warm, woman.
Have you family?"

She gestures at the horizon and beckons
            nothing but air.

We move along the road and
within a few miles come across
another keening woman,
            a toddler asleep
            in her arms.

Owen and I slow down.
Daddy doesn't stop this time
and when we've rounded the corner
says, "We can't help the whole country."

PART 6
January 1847

Removing the Roofs

At first it seems like just another morning,
the sky dense
               and dark with cloud.

Then Owen tumbles into the cottage—
"Come quickly!" he says—
               and out again like a bull.

Mammy jumps up.
        Daddy too.
And together we follow Owen.

Twenty-two children,
six women,
and four men
are standing outside their cottages
watching
              —motionless—
as gluttonous flames eat up
their thatched roofs
and spray the ground with
orange cinders.

It looks like a dragon has attacked,
but Saint Finnbarr slew
all the fire-breathers centuries ago.

"Why are they burning the roofs?"
Owen asks my father.

"They don't want people returning
when the bailiff's back is turned," he says.

"And Wicken wants the land to raise cattle.
He's replacing people with animals.
They'll pay for their keep," I add.
Daddy turns to look at me,
surprised I know all this.

Outside one of the cottages
Gilly McElligott is wailing
and clawing at the bailiff.
"Where are we meant to live?"

He kicks her away like she's nothing
more than a dog.

"Maybe it'll teach you all to
depend on yourselves from now on
and not the generosity of the landlord."

Rose is next to her mother,
        paralyzed.

I drift over.

"My grandfather built that cottage,"
Rose says matter-of-factly.

Mammy helps Gilly
gather her cups and spoons into a
woolen blanket.

"They'll stay with us
until we're all evicted," Rose says.
"We haven't paid rent either, so I'm sure we're next.
And then it's the workhouse for all of us."

I take her hand.
"Don't say that. What can I do?" I ask.

Rose snatches back her hand,
stares boldly at me.
"I hope your English friends
are pleased with themselves.
How can you stand to
be in that house with
Wicken, Nell?
                    He's a monster.
You wouldn't do this to a mongrel."

Mothers hold their pale, scrawny
children in their arms,
fathers collect up any belongings

they've managed to salvage,
but then they all
simply stand there,
nowhere to go,
homeless now,
                and hungry.

"Where will they live?" I ask Daddy.

He shakes his head.
He doesn't have any answers.
No one has.

The Witness

Wicken sits tall on horseback,
        watching the flames
        from a safe distance.

And once the houses
have turned into smoking
skeletons,
he kicks the horse
with his heels
and trots away
like he's just seen
something totally unremarkable.

And
following not far behind
on a brown horse
I see someone else.

Johnny Is with Him

Johnny is with him
and mesmerized
as he witnesses the roofs burn,
my friends' homes ablaze,
forced   out
          and the winter
here.

He does nothing.

He just follows his uncle
      back
      up
to The Big House.

What Could He Have Done?

Something.

Surely.

I mean
he could have done
something
to stop it.

Johnny Says . . .

"What exactly could I have done
aside from piss on the flames myself?
I begged my uncle to stop, Nell.
He asked me to take a ride
around the estate with him,
and that's what he showed me.
When I asked what they'd done to deserve it,
he said they were trespassing on his property."

"They aren't criminals.
They worked this land for generations."

"I know that. I'm not an idiot.
He said they hadn't paid their rents.
That was all they'd done.
He said he had to make the estate start
paying for itself. He's running out of money."

"He bought cases of champagne not long ago."
I know I am shouting.
I know it isn't Johnny's fault.
I can't stop.
"Is Rose next? My friend Rose?"

"I don't know who's next.
But he's not someone you can push around.
He's not even someone you can reason with.
He says it's not personal.
It's money and he's tried for years to make
it work as it is. I'm sorry, Nell.
I don't know what else to say."

An Offering

Johnny tries to walk me home
after work,
but I definitely
can't be seen with him now,
       not ever.
It's even more risky than before.

He hands me a parcel
wrapped in oilcloth.
"For your friends," he says.
"There's a pork joint in it.
No substitute for their home, but . . ."

"Thank you," I say. "You'll be beaten if
he finds out."

"There's one in there for your family too."

I nod and he kisses me gently.

I do not want his pity.
But I'm glad of the parcel.

By the Wall

I leave the pork
for the McElligotts
on the stone wall
outside Rose's hastily built cottage
so I don't have to talk
to anyone.

Rose sees me.
She doesn't come
outside,
doesn't ask me
in.

She turns away.

I've lost her.
I know that.

What else
will I lose before
the end of
all this?

Fever

Owen shivers and coughs,
though Mammy
has wrapped him tight in blankets.
His little tummy is distended.

"See what Gilly's got for a fever, Nell," Mammy says.

My brother whispers, "Am I dead already?
Are they taking me to be buried at the church?"

I kiss my brother's clammy forehead.
"You're not well, Owen.
But we'll make you better."

Rose's younger siblings are milling in her yard
like cattle in a pen on market day
but I can't see Rose or Eamon.

Gilly is by the door.
"Wicken hasn't burned the place
down yet, then?" I say.

"Not yet." Gilly sighs.

"Owen's got the fever," I tell her.

"Is it bad?"

"He has a swollen stomach."

"Right." She heads into the shed,
returns with a handkerchief.
"Put these herbs into a tea.
Have him drink it nice and hot.
And don't wrap him up if he's sweating.
Let him have air.
Open the door and let the fever out."
        She gets closer.
"Leave something outside for the good people
before yous go to sleep.
And say the rosary."

At home Owen is sitting up.
Mammy is holding him.
"He's not so bad," she says.
"He drank a little."

"I'm all right," he whispers.

"I'm glad," I say, tickling his feet,
which are   poking out
from the bottom of the blanket.
A part of me wants to kiss his toes.

"He's all right," Mammy repeats.

By Morning

By morning
Owen has managed to
drink a cupful of milk.

And all the seaweed
meant for the good people
is gone from the doorway.

The Devil

Mammy sits
in the corner, rocking Owen.
She kisses his forehead and says,
"He won't take water today."

I look up from my reading.

"Why isn't he hungry?" Mammy wonders.

"Did you give him the tea?" I ask.

"You mean he hasn't had anything
to drink at all?"
        Daddy wants to know.

"He's having a little nosebleed.
Get me a cloth to clean it, Nell," Mammy says.

Owen is not a whiner.
When he's hurt he'd rather
box you in the face
than show you he feels sore.
But he begins to moan.
A low sound that fills the room.

"Make him take more of that tea," I tell Daddy,
pushing open the door.

On the threshold I place another little
mound of seaweed for the good people
but as I am about to begin the rosary again
a magpie shoots by me and into the cottage.

"Get that devil out!" Mammy screams.
                "Get it OUT!"

We cannot.

And Daddy ends up killing the bird
with a pan to stop Mam's screams.

Plucked

We pluck and boil the magpie.
It's dead.
We might as well eat it.

Owen Recovers

Again he has roused himself,
recovered,
and we are making fun of one another.

It must be the tea.

Plus,
he is a little fighter.

"I'll save you something from my dinner," I tell him,
heading out for work
in the black of morning.

He gives me a grin.

Recovered.

Found

"You're not worried about
what the stable boy will think?"
I ask Johnny, straightening my dress.
"He'll know we were here. He'll suspect."

"Let him." Johnny traces lines in my palm.

"Please don't die," I say. "Don't leave me."

"I'm not dying. I'm not leaving.
You're stuck with me."
      He pulls me to him.
I wait for him to make a joke,
      lighten the moment with laughter.
"Promise *you* won't leave," he says.

I kiss him.
But I can't promise.

Johnny guides me to the stable wall,
his body against my hips to keep me there,
his mouth hungry,
fingertips against my face,
in my hair.

My own breath is dense,
my hands on his chest.

Then.
"Wait." I pull away.

He stops.
Straightaway he stops.
"Did you hear something?"

Suddenly there is scraping, knocking.

I expect to see
the stable boy
                or Silas.

Maggie Kennedy appears.
Without looking at us she says,
"Go home quickly, Nell.
Your brother has taken a bad turn.
My Eileen was just up to tell me."

I run—faster than I ever have before—
Johnny hurtling behind me.

"We should take a horse," he says.
"It'll be quicker."

When Owen Was Small

When Owen
was small
and Mammy and Daddy
were tending to the fields,
we would paddle by the shore
together
and catch crabs.

He screamed.
It felt so scary,
thrilling.

And bone-weary, I'd
carry him home
on my shoulders,
singing the whole
way.

When Owen
was small
there were happy times.

When Owen
was small.

Faster

We ride hard,
bumping
up and down
on the saddle,
my arms around
Johnny's waist.
"Faster," I cry.
"Go faster!"

Frozen

You'd think a sick boy would snivel
but Owen is as still as a
frozen river—
gurgling just beneath the ice,
      cold and quiet on top.

He seems small for a boy of ten,
      takes up so little room
      in the cottage
      compared to weeks ago
      when his flapping limbs knocked
      into everything,
      bothered everyone.

We all want warm milk
but Owen refuses.

Mammy shakes him awake
and that works for a minute or two
until Owen closes his eyes again
like he is tired with life.

"Wake up, my baby boy," Mammy whispers,
nuzzling her nose into Owen's neck.

She starts to sing,
      gently so only he can hear her.

Under her breath, Gilly McElligott
chants spells to appease the fairies,
          her eyes closed,
               waving a cross before her
               like a wand.

The rest of us drop to our knees:
"'*Hail Mary, full of grace,*
the Lord is with thee,'"
we chant,
and it sounds, somehow,
more like a curse
than a blessing.

Daddy nips my elbow.
"Run and get the doctor."

"There is no doctor," I tell him.

Surely he remembers.
But it happened so long ago.

Daddy bangs his fist against the wall.
"The priest, then.
Go and fetch Father Liam. Now!"

Johnny is waiting outside,
"The priest," I say,
climbing back on to the horse.

When the priest opens his door
I am panting. "Owen, my brother.
My brother Owen is deadly sick."

Father Liam blesses himself.
"I haven't the means to save him.
Only Christ himself has that power.
Come in and rest yourself a moment."

Johnny is behind me.
"I'm John Browning,
Lord Wicken's nephew.
Help her," he demands.

Better Now?

Daddy is leaning
against the doorway
with Bobby McElligott,
his head pressed
against the frame.

I dismount the horse,
and Johnny
ties the animal to the gate
while the priest
trots into the yard
on his donkey.

"Is Owen better?" I ask.
"Did he take any of the milk?
Is he better now?"

Gilly comes
out of the cottage
and shakes her head,
puts a hand
on my father's arm.

And
I fall to my knees,
knowing
I am
too late.

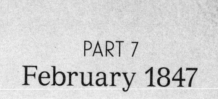

PART 7
February 1847

Consecrated Ground

The day after Owen dies
we take him to the churchyard.
The clay is frozen so solid,
an axe won't make a mark in the dirt.
Besides, there is no space.

Father Liam says,
"I'm sorry. There's no room
even for a coffin-less boy.
They've opened consecrated sites in Killala
where you could take him."

Bobby McElligott mutters,
"That's a mass grave. You don't expect . . ."

"It's not my doing," says the priest quickly.

"I'm taking him home," Daddy announces.

"The ground must be consecrated," Father Liam
            calls after us.

"Fuck off with yourself
and your fucking consecrated ground,"
Daddy shouts back.

By the Old Oak Tree

Daddy, Bobby, and Eamon
spend the day digging—
a lonely hole not far
from the old oak tree
in our very own yard.

What Else?

Gilly makes tea with herbs and helps tidy up.
"Can I do anything else, Mary?" she asks.

Mammy looks up.
Her eyes are empty.

"What else is there to do?" she asks.

This Wailing

It is impossible
to stifle the sound of sobbing and coughing
in our small cottage.

Mammy shudders and sniffs
late into the night.

"How can I help her?" I ask Daddy.

"Let her cry," he tells me.

I used to hear my parents sometimes,
        giggling
        in the darkness,
and wished the noise of it away,
mortified by what I knew
was happening
beneath their blankets.

But this wailing is worse.

Questions

Daddy wants to know
why Johnny rode me home
the day Owen died—
      what drove him
        to such compassion.
And he waited. He seemed to care.

I cannot speak.

If I do, I will have to tell the truth
        and it's the last
thing I want to admit to my father.

"He made you that little figurine, didn't he,
the English boy?"

"He did, Daddy."

"It won't end well, Nell. For us or for them."

"What do you mean?"

My father clears his throat vaguely,
like the scratch of a bullet in the barrel of a gun.
"Things are changing.
It's a famine now. A deep hunger is here.
And trouble is coming."

Without Owen

Mammy gazes at the wall,
sticky with grief.

The sunrise does not rouse her,
        nor my murmurs
for her to have some tea.

Daddy sits before the fire
warming his bare feet,
his head bent,
his beard growing long.

I'm not surprised.

Why would they want another glimpse
of this world without Owen in it?

Back at The Big House

"How did he die?" Maggie asks
when I finally drag myself
back to work.

She takes my hand, presses it
like she is kneading dough.
It is the first time she has ever been tender with me.

"Typhoid," I tell her,
though I can't make sense of it.

Maggie says,
"Your poor mother."

I cannot help it.
        I fall against her,
        screaming all my pain
        into her shoulder.

She wraps her arm around my waist.
"Oh, Nell. Nell, it's fine.
It's going to be fine."

I sit up, eyeball her.

"*Who* is going to be fine?
You? Me? Our thieving landlord?"

"*Shh*. He'll hear you."
She pulls at the sleeves of her dress.
"You're very thin, Nell.
Have you slept at all?"

I shake my head.

"And you should eat something."

Maggie slices a bit of bread
from the warm loaf on the range
and lathers it in butter and marmalade.

But I can't touch it.

I can't even look
at food.

Right in Front of Me

While I was carrying on with Johnny
my brother was being coaxed
into the afterlife.

He was dying
right in front
of me.

But I was so wrapped up in something else
I wasn't at home to help.

I thought a fever
could be fixed with hot tea and humor.

I thought Owen would get well.

      I'd stopped listening to him.
      Cuddling him.
Making him my favorite.

All our lives are threatened.
But I didn't want to see it.

"I can't be with you anymore,"
I tell Johnny and he nods,
understanding.
Understanding
more than most

because of what happened to Charlie
and his father.

But before he leaves the kitchen
he says, "I'm still here.
I'm not going anywhere.
Anytime you need me."

Guilt

I know I'm not to blame for my brother's death
and Johnny isn't to blame either,
but
that doesn't dull the guilt
every time
I remember
my brother's narrow face
the last time I saw him
alive
or my mother's voice
as she sang him into sleep.

Charlatan

A stranger arrives,
a trader without any pigs
or chickens in his wagon.
There's no sidestepping dung
or warming our hands
on brown freckled farm eggs
when he rolls into Ballinkeel—
he is selling spells:

> bottles of green and red elixirs,
> magic "that will make the potatoes
> new again." he says.
> "Tonics that will bring your babies
> back to life."

I wish I had something to sell
so we could pour a potion
over the ground where
we buried Owen and
see if his dead body sprouts.

But Mammy drags me away,
her face a storm,
her eyes filled with tears.
She tells me not to be taken in.
"That man is a wretch," Mammy warns,
playing with the pin in her shawl,
trying to keep her composure.

She can't.
She runs back.
She hammers him with her fists,
      snatches his potions,
      and pitches them
      against the schoolyard wall,
      the glass shattering,
          scattering.

"Go!" she screeches.
"Get out of our village, you charlatan.
How dare you come here
with your diabolical promises and lies?
Get out of here!"

The man gathers up his things
but is not deterred,
tries again nearer the church.

Father Liam is having none of it,
finally runs him from the village
by swatting the stranger
with his leather-bound Bible
and leveling God's curses at him.

But there are some who follow him,
who still want to see,
to know if there really is

a potion to turn the potatoes around.
Holy water isn't working.
And neither is hope.
Or waiting.
Or leaving gifts out for the fairies.

Mammy and I go home and
boil a small turnip and onion for supper
that we bought with my wages.

We all eat in silence,
trying not to think about
the charlatan or
Owen beneath
the oak tree in the yard.

Leaving

"We're moving to Dublin.
There's nothing here for us.
We have to go," Rose says.

"It's hours away," I say.

"I wanted to say goodbye," she replies.

She is clutching a
bunch of dried flowers.

We drift outside to where
Owen is buried and lay
them next to the tree.

"I wish we hadn't fallen out," I say.
"I've needed a friend."

"I think you have one," she says,
but without cruelty.

"Not anymore.
Not after what's happened."

Rose blesses herself and mumbles a prayer.
"Maybe this English lad is your way
out of here. To England or America.
Maybe he's a way out for all of you."

She puts her arms around me,
holds on tight.
"Eamon can't cope with goodbyes.
He told me to say he'll miss you.
And to be careful."

"Do you have to leave?"
Rose and I half smoked our first pipe together,
told stories as we hunted for duck eggs,
gossiped about Eamon
and all the other boys
through the night.

"We have to grow up. It's time," she says.

I know this is true,
I'm not naive.
But I don't want to lose
anyone else.

"Maybe you'll come to Dublin yourself soon.
In the spring?
There's work there for scullery maids.
But not for the fancy girls of aristocrats."

She kisses me quickly
and is gone,
                not glancing
                back
                once.

By the River

I wait by the river,
hoping Johnny will show up.

By chance
or design.

I wait,
not knowing how
I'd react if I saw him.

But the light fades
and the stippled water
is dark.

      He does not come.

The world is silent
         and cold.

Being Loved

It got to me.
Being loved.
Knowing he was longing for me.

Somewhere
not far from here
Johnny is breathing,
blood running through
each limb,
all the way to his toes
        and fingertips.

In bed I clutch my left hand
        with my right,
imagine he is the one holding it.

But he is not here now.
He is not mine.

I have pushed him away
and it has worked—
        he has heard me.

I only have myself to blame for that.

Not Here

Mammy is up to her elbows in water,
hands wrestling with rags.
"I can do that," I say,
but she swats me away.
     "I'm doing it."
     Her hair is lank, dirty.
     She is wearing no shoes,
         her feet soiled.

When she's done washing,
she spreads the bits
over the bramble bushes
though it's bitter out
and there'd be a better chance
of drying in the cottage.

The rags are Owen's clothes—
     his tatty trousers, tiny vests.

I imagine him
     watching from the far side of the yard,
     tucking his hands into his armpits
     and heading off,
     marching hard.

When the clothes are dry and folded,
piled on a stool by the fire like a cushion,
Mammy says,

"Take those bits to the Doyles
and give them to a child who needs them."

I lay them on my lap, sit next to Mammy.
We are quiet for a long time.
"Whatever happened
with the English boy?" she asks.

"We aren't friends anymore."

"Why's that?"

I stroke the hem of Owen's trousers.

He liked to hide
        and have you find him;
        it could take hours
        and end in an argument.
        He would have been handsome
                had he lived.
        He had plump lips.

"You couldn't have changed things, Nell.
Owen was sick."

"I wasn't here."

Mammy scrapes her stool against the floor,
        comes closer.
She smells of soot.

"It seems like you still aren't here, Nell.
It seems like you're still somewhere else.
Very far away from us all."

I press Owen's trousers to my chest.

> I wish he were hiding
> so I could look for him.

I wish I could find him.

A Small Boy with Curls

I dream I am searching.
First I find Owen,
swollen-stomached and crying.
Then Johnny is there
holding us both,
                    making it better.

I wake before the birds
and by the door
find a packet—
another wooden carving wrapped in paper.

I squeeze the little figure tight in my fist:
                    a small boy with curls.

Alive

I go into Wicken's yard
to thank Johnny for the carving.
He is talking to a laborer,
does not come close to me.

The laborer leaves and Johnny remains
at a distance
          giving me all   the   space
          I asked for,
not knowing it isn't
what I want anymore.

I go to him.
"Please wait until I'm dead
to find someone else," I say.

He smiles. "I'd kindly request the same."

Horse hooves sound behind me.
Johnny's eye widen.
"Uncle," he says.

I turn, bow.
"Good afternoon, Lord Wicken."

"Ellen Quinn," he says.
"Helping with the building work now, are you?"

"She was asking about supper, Uncle.
Mrs. Kennedy has cooked a rabbit."

The landlord looks unimpressed.
"How are your parents?" he asks with formality.

"Alive."

The horse steps sideways,
          brays into brackish air.
"I'm glad to hear that," he says.

Alive.

No longer a pithy reply
but a sad statement of fact.

I Do Not Want to See

Mammy is perched on a mound of grass
at the edge of our land.

Her teeth chatter.
Her body twitches.
She will not reply to questions,
jabbers unintelligibly until I shake her
into sense and she looks at me.
"A baby. It was just born," she mutters.
"A baby girl just born."

"What baby, Mammy?
What's happened?"

"I was on my way up to see Gilly.
It was just lying naked in a pile of brambles.
I had to run. I couldn't see it."

"It was a puppy, Mammy.
It must have been a puppy."

Her lips are white.
She shakes her head furiously.
"It was a brand-new baby.
The head was scratched
like an owl had attacked it.
Do you think her mother abandoned her?
Or killed her?

Some women are killing babies
if they can't feed them."

I wrap her in my arms.
I do not ask her to show me or tell me more.

I do not want to see.
I do not want to know.

Last Supper

Mammy gives each of us
a dollop of cornmeal
bought last week,
again with my wages.

Daddy sits quietly,
something brewing in him.

Our stomachs cramp from hunger.

Mammy doesn't say it,
but this is the last of the food.

She never lets me feel responsible
for feeding everyone.

But I am.

I have been for some time now.

At Dusk

At dusk Johnny knocks.
I open the squeaking door to him.
He is a silhouette against the night.
"Who is it, Nell?" Mammy calls out.
Johnny's hair is swept neatly to one side.
Warmth somehow bleeds into the cottage.
He hands me a handkerchief
heavy with oats.

I pass the package to Mammy.
"I'll be back soon," I say.

He takes my hand
right there in the yard and says,
"At night I can hear your voice."

"What am I saying?" I ask,
leading him away so Daddy won't see us.

"You're saying you need me.
So I'm here. I want to be here."

"I smell you," I tell him.
"*And* I hear your voice.
It's very serious.
So is your laugh.
I never knew anyone
with a serious laugh before."

He nods.
"Before I met you, I was numb.
         I felt nothing.
         Now I feel too much."

I nod then,
and we walk up the lane,
strange flies circling,
surviving the cold better than people.

"I don't even know what you do with your days.
I used to know your every movement," he says.

I start to cry.

Johnny presses my face between his palms.
"The hurt is so much when I don't have you,
I wonder whether being in love is
worth the pain that goes with it."

"I didn't mean to hurt you," I tell him.
"I really didn't mean to hurt you."

No More

While Mammy sleeps,
Daddy studies maps.

Not grand globes like those Master Sweeney
used to show us in the schoolroom
but small hand-drawn scratchings
easily folded and hidden in his pocket.

"What are you doing?" I ask.

He reaches for his flat cap.
"Feeding God-knows-who
and God-knows-where
with our grain
when the country is starving," he says.
"No more of my family or friends
are going to die.
The fever and the famine can go to hell."
He hands me my coat.
"Well, are you coming?"

The Gathering

I recognize all the men
gathered in the churchyard.
    Some are neighbors,
    some of them are Daddy's friends:
    Bobby McElligott
    and Murphy the blacksmith.
"Sit there, and if anyone comes
along the road, you cough a fit.
And I mean anyone at all," Daddy says.

I sit on a stone, an oil sack covering my head to
keep the rain at bay.
My skirt sticks to my legs.

There is murmuring,
urgent words,
but the men are careful to keep
        their voices low.

Back home Mammy says,
    "Where were yous?
    It's a horrible night out."

Daddy glances at me.

It is a look that seals a secret.
"I had a nip of drink with the boys.
We're saving a bit by not bothering with Mass

and I needed it, Mary.
A man needs a nip
        now and then.
            A woman needs one too."

"And where were *you*?"
Mammy is frowning
at my wet clothes,
my hair dripping on the floor.
She doesn't quite believe Daddy,
who has never been a man for the drink.

"I was waiting in case Daddy hadn't
his walking legs on him afterwards.
I heard a lot of singing.
A lot of dreadful singing."

"I am not a great singer.
But as you see,
I walk very well," Daddy says.
He jumps, knocks the soles of his boots together.
The fire sniffs.

"Get to bed the both of you," Mammy says.
"And no more spending on poteen
until we've all eaten a pile of rashers.
You hear me?
I'll thrash you both if you disobey me."

Daddy salutes like he might actually be drunk.
"Yes, Captain," he says.
"Permission to come in for a kiss, Captain."

Mammy's nostrils flare,
and a smile,
the first one in weeks.
"Get to bed," she says.
"I'll have no more nonsense."

Every Day

There are piles of people
dropping dead
every day.

They simply wither up
and fall down,
     give way
           to death.

There seems a simple solution
to all the starvation:
        if many die there are
        less to feed
        and fewer Irish
        people in Ireland
        at least.

People are using the word *murder*
and what else would you call it
when they're feeding corn to cows?

What would you call it
when we're starving
in the midst of plenty?

Everything

Johnny comes for me at nighttime,
pushes my hair from my face
and we talk about everything.

In the daytime
we have to be careful,
and in any case
I am
too exposed
by the light to tell
him how I feel.

But at night,
in the shadows,
truth and touching
seem so much easier.

Turnaround

"It's none of my business,
but he's a lovely boy, isn't he?
Isn't he lovely for an Englishman?" Maggie says.

He Is

Yes.

An Irishman

The cold makes my spine hurt,
my back bend.
Daddy and the men are growling,
        audible arguments erupting occasionally
into a few faint phrases.
        And get arrested?
        Arrested? We'll be hanged.
        My children are dying.
        My wife can't get out of the bed.
        Better to hang than starve.

I am so intent on spying, I don't
spot a figure on the road
until he is upon me,
looming, louring.
"Ah, I see, Nell Quinn. Of course.
So you're their lookout."

I do as I have been instructed,
                cough hard,
                let out a yelp.
But the men are loud,
too busy bickering to hear me.

Father Liam rolls his eyes,
        squares his shoulders,
        strides past me.

"Daddy!" I call out,
following the priest. "Daddy!"

The men turn from their circle,
        about a dozen in dark clothes
        each holding a tool:
        spade, hoe, wrench.

"Gentlemen," the priest says.

"Father Liam," they mutter.

Daddy eyes me. Inclines his head.
        But I'm going nowhere.

"There are rumors," Father Liam says.
"I've come to check on the hearsay.
I'm sure I don't believe it."

Murphy, dressed in a tattered gray overcoat,
shifts his weight from one foot to the other.
"Do we need to silence you, Father?"

Daddy rests a hand on the blacksmith's shoulder.
"Settle down, Murphy."

The other men shift uncomfortably.
In the distance a baby cries.
The wind rips through my clothes.

Bobby McElligott pipes up.
"We haven't a choice, Father."

"If yous don't put down those weapons
no sacrament will absolve you.
No God will forgive you."

It is Daddy's turn to address to the priest.
"No innocent will come to harm, Father.
No woman. No child . . ." He pauses.
"And no Catholic.
All we ask is that you mind your council.
Think no more on it, and if you do,
pray for our victory."

"Go *home*!"
The priest's voice is thunderous.
Some of the men move toward him.
I flatten my body into the hedge.

The distant baby cries louder
and I am reminded of that stormy night,
the threat of banshee and resulting blight.

"A ship leaves this week," Daddy explains.
"It'll be crammed full of the oats

Wicken and others have been buying up
          and stockpiling."

"The oats yous grew left long ago, man.
Be sensible."

"People are starving on this island.
We won't see food sent across the sea, Father.
I'm sorry, but you've a wasted trip.
Come on now, boys."

The group follows Daddy and Bobby,
one of them knocking the priest aside
with his shoulder.
From the darkness more men appear,
          perhaps another five,
          each carrying a scowl
          as well as a weapon.

"I will not take your confession!" the priest shouts.

Murphy hangs back.
"But you won't be tattling either.
And you know why not, Father?
Because you're a clergyman all right.
But you're also an Irishman.
And that, I know, runs very deep."

Untold

I stop telling Johnny everything;
I cannot reveal Daddy's meetings
with the other men.
I consider it.
Because I trust Johnny
        absolutely.
But it would be too great
        a betrayal.

Prayer

Father Liam leans on the gate,
his mouth aslant.
"Where is your father?"

                    I shrug.

"And your mother?"

                    "Inside."

The priest's Adam's apple bobs up and down.
He puts his hands into the folds of his tunic.
"I was surprised to see you last night
with the men, Nell."

I step closer to him so he will lower his voice,
                so Mammy won't hear.
"No need to be getting a girl
involved in these things.
I presume they want to use you somehow?"

"How do you mean, Father?"

"Well, you working up at The Big House and all.
What is your involvement?"

"I haven't been told, Father," I admit,
and for the first time
I consider this—
the possibility
that Daddy will have a job for me.

Father Liam sighs,
cranes his neck for me to hear,
but stays on the far side of the gate.
"The last thing we want are soldiers
from the barracks in Killala
here in our village.
Tell your father to stop what he's at.
Surely you have some way
to persuade him."

"Mammy's the only person he'd listen to."

"And she doesn't know," he says.

"Truth be told, since Owen died
she'd be likely to encourage Daddy."

"I've a terrible feeling," he says,
not really addressing me now,
looking north toward the bay.

Ravens swoop and caw.

"I'll pray for yous.
I'll pray for your father."

Accomplice

Nonchalantly Daddy asks,
"Where do they store the oats
up at The Big House?"

"Next to the coal sheds," I say.
"Behind the pigpens.
But only the oats Wicken's men
harvested themselves."

"That's not what I've heard," Daddy says.
"He's storing more than his share."
I don't contradict him.
"Do the dogs know you now?" he continues.

"What do you mean, Daddy?"

"Do they bark when you approach
or are they friendly?"

"They run to me, their tails wagging."

"All the dogs? Even the fiercest?"

"All the dogs, Daddy."

"Very good," he says. "Very good."

On My Mind

Wicken is in Westport with Major Chambers,
so Johnny and I feed the geese by the pond
without too much worry.
"You're quiet," he says.
"Is there something on your mind?"

Johnny chews a fingernail.
His lips are full, his cheeks red,
he hasn't the pinched look of most people.

"I have a fair bit on my mind," I say.
"But if I tell you, you'd be involved.
You definitely don't want
anything to do with what's looming."

"Maybe I could help."

"Could you convince your uncle
to give the oats he's storing to his tenants?"

"Nell . . ."

"I know.
I've seen the boar's head on the wall.
Wicken is a man who sticks spears into
animals for sport. No mercy.
It would be pointless for you to ask."

Across the yard Silas is shaking
a small rug
and using a cane to smack
the dirt from it.
"Is he bothering you?" Johnny asks.

"He hasn't been near me," I say.

We do not discuss the oats again.

No One Will Get Hurt

"Wake up," Daddy whispers.

I edge away from Mammy's back
that smells of bracken
          and follow Daddy as he
          slinks into the night.

He roots around the turf shed,
then heads along the road.

I run to catch up.
The sting of cold is in my knuckles.

"Where are the others?" I ask.

"Hurry up, pet. Come on."

After a while
we arrive at The Big House—
of course,
                    where else?

Johnny's window is lit up,
a smell of coal comes from a chimney.

Everything else is still.

We crawl through a fracture in the fencing
and Daddy hands me some slithers of meat.

"All you've to do is attract the dogs and
lead them down the lane."

"Where did you get the meat, Daddy?"

He doesn't reply to the question, says,
"Take them as far away as you can.
Across the river and north."

"They have dogs in the house too, Daddy."

"We aren't going near the house," he says.
        I feel my body release,
        a fear punctured.
"We're twenty men strong.
We can carry two bags of oats apiece."

"No one will get hurt? You promise?"

"We aren't intending anyone any harm.
Down to the shore, remember?
Meet me back at the cottage."

"Daddy . . ."
It hits me what is happening
and what the punishment
will be if my father is caught.
"Don't do it. We'll find a way through."

"Get rid of the dogs, Nell."

Innocent

The hounds growl,
pummel the ground, and
snarf at the wind
when I whistle to them.

I wave the scraps
by their noses
and they sniff,
their jowls sloppy.

I ruffle their wiry coats
and playfully they
gnaw at my meaty fists.

I take them along
the lane toward the river
leading to the bay,
where the gulls
are already wheeling
in the early-morning
murk.

The dogs yap in pleasure
at this unexpected adventure.

And then
we come upon a man.
Sissy Doyle's nephew, Declan.

He has a gun.
"I'll take them from here, Nell," he says.

The dogs growl
and look at me for
reassurance.

I stroke their muzzles
and shush them.

Declan has a length
of rope over his arm.
"Will they set upon me?" he asks.

"They're innocent," I say.

"Will they attack me?"
He is impatient.

"Now we're away from the grounds,
I don't think so."

Declan puts out his hand
and I pass him the
bits of meat.

He stomps away
and the dogs follow,
unsure.

"Go home, girl."

Long After

Daddy arrives
home long after I do.
"Into bed," he whispers.

He is coughing
     and breathless,
     struggles out of his
     own clothes
     as fast as he can.
"We've been here
     all night," he says.
"Asleep.
     We've been here
     all night."

On Their Way

Murphy's knock is deafening.
And he is panting,
sweat beading on his mustache.
"Where's your father?"
He pushes past me into the cottage.
"Michael."

Daddy jumps up quickly.
"They're coming?"

Murphy nods. "They cut by my place.
So it's you or O'Connell they're after."

"How much time have I got?" Daddy asks.

Murphy shakes his head. "They're on horseback."

"Go *now*, Daddy.
Don't just stand there!"
I hand him his jacket,
        scramble to find his boots.

Murphy turns and is gone as quickly as he came.
Daddy puts on his cap.

Dogs bark in the distance.
Not the hounds.
They've been killed, surely?

And Mammy is putting on her coat.
"What's all the fuss?" she asks.
"What did Murphy want at this hour?
Michael? Are you all right?"

The Arrest

Daddy doesn't put up any fight.

"Don't hurt my girls," is all he says
to the men wearing red jackets,
wielding guns.

Mammy won't shut up.

The men pin her to the wall.
"Get your filthy hands off me."
She squeals Daddy's name,
"Michael! Michael!"
then desperately claws at the wall
as though lost in a forest
and looking for him.

"I'm all right, Mary," Daddy says
as his hands are tied together with twine.
"I didn't hurt anyone," he says to me.
"I swear on Owen's soul."

"What do you mean, Daddy?"

A redcoat drags my father to the road by his hair.

"Here it is," another soldier says.
"As we thought,"
as a third lugs the bags of oats

over the wall
where they were hidden in the rotten field.

They don't put Daddy up on a horse
with the grain.
They tie the rope to a saddle
and he must trot to keep up.
He looks like a pig being led to market
        on a leash,
to be sold as meat.

Mammy kneels in the yard
close to Owen's burial spot,
punching the dirt
and howling Daddy's name.
"Get up, Mammy," I beg.

But she can't.

Hurt

Daddy promised no one
would be hurt
but somehow
Lord Wicken
heard the commotion
in the outbuilding
as the men stole
the oats and
when he went to see
what was going on was
battered across the head
and injured.

So the crime isn't theft now,
    because the perpetrator
    went for Wicken's head.
Daddy will be tried
for attempted murder.

In the Drove Way

I do not risk
going up to The Big House.

I loiter by a hedgerow
near the gatepost for a long time
until Johnny sees me,
rushes down the drove way.
I run up to meet him midway.

"My uncle is demented with rage.
He's after blood," he says.

"He's alive at least."

"He was up and about within hours.
But he's been humiliated.
And he's ready for vengeance."

"He wants my father's neck
but Daddy didn't touch your uncle.
He swore to me that he didn't
hurt anyone."

"My uncle can't remember much.
Silas was the one who picked out
your father."

"Was Silas there?"

"Upstairs watching
from a window. apparently."

"No guts to go down
and defend his employer?
He's worse than a rat.
He should be afraid of *me* now.
If I catch up with him
I won't be responsible for
what becomes of him."

Johnny presses his hand to my cheek.
"You can't be back at work.
My uncle would kill you.
But I'll come to you every day."

"He'll be hanged."

"He won't. I'll think of something."

Beneath the Clear

I don't feel embarrassed
when I take off my tattered dress
in front of Johnny
and step into the river.

Though it's freezing,
the sun is out for once,
and all I want is a little
water to wash over me,
to shock something
out of my system.

Johnny watches me rub the water
over my skinny ribs and hips
and
       when I step out
wraps me in a blanket
and we lie together
beneath the clear,
unfed sky.

The Shipment

If they're going to take the trouble to
               send something
               across the sea
they'd be as well to send something we need.

What we need is grain.
Grain or potatoes.
Grain or potatoes or cabbage.

What we really need is food.

What we don't need are guns.
What we don't need are soldiers.

Yet that's what we have been sent.

A troop of fresh redcoats
spilled from the
bowels of a boat in Killala Bay yesterday.

They're here to protect the grain.
They're here to protect
        food from being stolen by people like Daddy.
They're here to protect
        people like Lord Wicken
        from coming to any harm.
They have to put a halt to food riots.

We need food
but instead
they sent a swarm of soldiers.

Lumpy Leather

Gilly McElligott says,
"We're away to Canada."
Then she whispers in Mammy's ear,
but the only word I hear is "Bobby."

The McElligotts are never coming back.
They have sold all they own,
including the stolen oats, and are
running from the famine.

Who would blame them?

Mammy gives Gilly our only satchel.
It isn't much—a lumpy leather thing
Owen and I slept in as babies—
bumped and bruised
like it's been beaten up.
        The locks are rusted over.

"Bobby won't be caught," I say,
once Gilly is out the door.
"He gets to scurry off like some little weasel
while Daddy's sitting there in his cell.
Was Bobby the one who battered Wicken?"

Mammy reaches for my father's pipe,
                              lights it.
"Fairness doesn't come into it.

This world operates on injustice.
Can you imagine if they invested as much
in saving people's lives
as they do on keeping people down?
It'll take a new generation to fight.
Those of us left are too tired to pick up a spade,
let alone a gun.
But I tell you this:
if they execute your father
they might as well hang *me*.
Find a rope and tie me to it."

"Mammy! Don't talk like that," I say,
wanting to smack her.

"Kill me too!" she shouts.

Books for Keeps

Johnny is weighed down with jars.
"My uncle is adamant
about the gallows," he says,
bundling his donations on to the table:
jams, pickles, a piece of ham.

From each pocket he retrieves a small book
        and carefully places both of them
next to a stack of washed rags.

Mammy is not at home.
She walks early in the mornings
when I am still asleep.

"How's your father?"

"We're not allowed to see him," I explain,
talking into the table.

"They're claiming that
he was the mastermind behind it," Johnny says.

"I have no idea," I reply, which is true.

He shuffles, fingers the food.
"You mustn't despair," he says.

And I'm trying.

I'm really trying hard
to hang on.

Come With Us

Mammy and I are tucked up in bed
when Gilly McElligott
comes banging at the door
like a bailiff.

"Open up! I haven't long!"

Mammy gets up, grumbling.

"There's been a change of plan,"
Gilly McElligott hisses.
Her voice is still full of the night-wind.
"My aunt Annie died.
Poor soul is gone with the fever.
She had no one
and was to come with us, Mary."
        And then:
"We've a ticket now for your Nell.
And you should let her leave.
There's no use anyone staying.
You know I'd care for your girl.
Rose and Eamon will join us next year too,
please God."

Nothing moves.

Even the mice in the chimney stay still,
waiting for the verdict.

Mammy wobbles in the doorway.

Gilly McElligott has to hold her up.
"I haven't long." She lowers her voice.
"Bobby is waiting down by the bay."

I know Mammy is thinking she should send me.
It would be the kindest thing.
To put me on that ship.
A new life.

"If she's coming, she'll have to get up
and gather her bits," Gilly McElligott says.

Mammy moves toward me,
sits on her heels.
"You can go. I wouldn't blame you.
I wouldn't blame you one little bit," she says.
"It's up to you, Nell."

As If I Would Go

As if.

Half-Family

We are split in two,
not the same family
we were anymore.

We have lost Owen and Daddy.

Divided.

We are a half-family.
Broken.

So
I have to keep what remains
together.

In Court

We are crammed like animals
into a courtroom for the trial.

The public murmur and grumble
in Irish so the officials can't understand
their complaints of corruption.

I do not like the smell;
something combining
a pigpen with church:
shit and wax.

Judge Grey is a thousand years old
in a worn gray wig.
He has an eye-patch
and patches too on the elbows of his gown,
a well-worn man who is
not pleased to be here:
his frown is deep
and dark.

Daddy is marched into the courtroom in handcuffs.
He glances across at us, tests out a smile.
"Michael," Mammy whispers, wringing her shawl.

The questioning begins,
a man dressed in tight trousers
pointing at Daddy, accusing him

of assault,
stealing,
ringleading,
attempted murder of the landlord.

Silas Simmons answers only one question:
"Did you see this man the night
Lord Wicken was beaten and left for dead?"
And he replies, "I did, sir."

Daddy doesn't have a lawyer,
only Father Liam,
who has known Daddy
twenty years and can vouch for him.
"He wouldn't kick a stray," the priest says.
But Father Liam is no match for the law
and when he begins to justify the theft,
reminding the court that Daddy lost a son,
that his family was hungry,
the judge interrupts,
spraying the court with spittle.

      "Life is a challenge,
      but not all men are thieves.
      Many work rather than starve.
Most families have received some form of relief.
      Lord Wicken himself has made vast donations
      to the poor.
      This indictment is another example
      of the ingratitude of the poor of this county
      who blame anyone but themselves."

He gulps deeply from a jug
     and I wonder
     whether it's water
     or something stronger.

Daddy isn't giving ear to Judge Grey,
seems to be blocking out the whole courtroom.

He has turned to Mammy.
They regard each other,
knowing nods passing between them
that no one else is meant to notice.
I want to tell him to concentrate.
I want to tell her to stop distracting him.
They should be listening, not sending love signals.

The priest sits and I assume Daddy
will be given a voice,
but the arguing is over—
     he does not defend himself
     on the witness stand.
     He remains silent,
     looks down at his handcuffs.

Lord Wicken doesn't speak either.
He watches from a corner of the courtroom,
     Johnny next to him, ashen.

Suddenly the judge has gone.
The courtroom noise is crushing.

Mammy and I grip one another.
Daddy looks beaten,
and maybe he has been:
it would explain the bruising.
"What's happening?" she asks,
pulling on my sleeve.

"We wait for a decision," I say.

"What? That's it?"
She pulls at me again.

Among the hubbub,
a redhead in a gray overcoat:
      Murphy.
      He is looking directly at me
      and in an instant
      I know it was him who hit
      the landlord.

I jostle for space and then
Johnny is at my side.
"It's so hard to get air," I tell him.
"Why won't they just let people breathe?"

"Let's go outside."

"What about your uncle?"

"He's gone for lunch with Judge Grey
and Major Chambers," he says.

Damned

Judge Grey's gavel hits the bench
with a bang and the word
Guilty.
Then a black cloth is placed
on the crown of his head.

We know what is coming.

My father is unshaken:
a strong man, brave, but
gentle as a butterfly.

The courtroom settles to a hush.
"I cannot overlook the facts.
You are a thief and a violent man
who attempted to murder
Lord Wicken, your landlord.
You planned the robbery
with more than a dozen men,
many of whom have evaded capture.
We must make an example of you."

The tick of a clock.
The whisper of an insect.

"Michael Quinn, ten days hence
you will be taken to a place of execution
and there hanged by the neck

until you are dead.
May God have mercy upon your soul."

I expect a curse at least,
but Mammy only croaks,
unable to utter another sound.
She elbows me
for an explanation, which I do not have.

Daddy is watching me.
There is a slow wink.
It is a signal.

It is all up to you now, Nell.

It is up to you to resist.

Michael Quinn

After the trial we are given a chance
to see my father in his cell
since he's not going to prison
for a couple of years
like most in here
but

       to the gallows.

The guards can't help feeling sorry for us,
offer up tins of hot gruel,
which we refuse.

The light in the cell feels like it is being
   sucked out
       through the buttonhole
       window above the straw bed.
Daddy's ankles have been chafed by chains.

I tell him about the onion seeds
I planted
up where the potatoes used to be.

And when Daddy offers me his hand
I shake my head,
unable to touch him.

It is too much.

"Maybe you'll sing?" Daddy asks.
"Or give us a poem.
That would be a real gift."

So I try.
I really do try.
I open my mouth
because my head is full of words.
But every time I open my mouth
the sound catches in my throat
and it all comes out a squawk.
   My neck is sore.

"Don't worry," Daddy says,
"you can sing on the road home
and I'll hear it through the window."

Too soon
guards are knocking
and Daddy is holding on to Mammy
like he will expire if he releases her.
She coughs,
snot running into her mouth.

   I take tiny breaths and
   lower my gaze.

"Nell, my love," Daddy says.
"My first baby."
   I feel his fingers reach for me
   but push his hand away.

"Your baby?" I shout,
staring now at this man
who is nothing like my father,
      reeking and skinny,
      shackled and defeated.
"It's your job to care for us, protect us.
And you're leaving it all to me!
I warned you. How *could* you?"

"Nell!" Mammy starts toward me.

Daddy holds her back.
"Nell," he whispers. "Come here."

"You should have ratted out the other men.
Murphy is a coward.
And Bobby.
Every one of them is willing
to let you swing."

"Nell . . ." His hand is on my elbow.

"You should have betrayed them all!" I scream.

"Nell," he repeats gently.
The light is gone from his eyes.
The bite from his spirit.

He wraps me in his arms.
I sob into his shoulder.
Three hopeless words appear in the air:

"Don't die, Daddy," I say.
And then:
"Please don't go."

Mammy presses in next to us,
her face flattened against us both.

"Always take risks," Daddy says.
"And live a big life.
You promise me you'll do that?"

"I promise," I mumble.

We stand apart and he takes me in.
"You're right. You're no baby, Nell.
You're some woman."

He smiles and straightens up.
Proud.
My father.

Michael Quinn.

Wilting

Mammy is barely holding on.
At night she curls herself into a tight
          ball and
screams into the blanket on the bed.

I try talking to
and holding her.
She still has me.
But I am not enough.

Mammy worshipped my father
like a pagan,
loving him
her whole life.

I cannot imagine
losing something like that.

With Owen and Daddy gone
I've no idea
how to make Mammy's life worth living.
She says, "What are you thinking about?"

"Nothing, Mammy," I say.
"What are *you* thinking about?"

"Nothing," she replies. "Nothing at all."

Murphy

Murphy twists his flat cap in his hands.
"I'm sorry for your trouble," he says.

Mammy hardly looks up.
"He isn't dead yet, Callum."

"And he didn't blab, Mary.
If he'd given us up
we'd all be for the gallows.
He's a man, to be sure."

Mammy stirs a pot on the fire.
"If they offered him a way out
I'd have encouraged him to talk
and let you swing
so he could come home to us."

Murphy scratches his head,
lays a stack of coins on the table
and is gone.

Reusable

The undertaker only makes reusable coffins now,
a trapdoor to release the dead into a lime pit.
> And rumors have it they sometimes
> release even the living into the lime.

The Doyles lost another child,
the youngest boy, last week.

It's deathdeathdeathdeath
no matter which way you look.

At Sunset

"Are you out of your mind?" Johnny shouts.

"Probably."

I march ahead of him.
At the bend in the road is
a decaying dog.
I try not to look,
finger the carrots in my apron:
a gift for the remaining Doyle children.

Johnny stamps his boot and clenches his fists.
The sun is beginning to set.

"Threatening guards with a weapon?
Do you know how well protected the barracks is?
They'll have the redcoats on you within minutes.
You won't succeed.
And you'll be *killed* for it.
You think they wouldn't let you hang
because you're a girl?
My uncle doesn't give a damn about you.
What he cares about are money and land and power.
I live with him. I *know* who he is."

"I won't be caught if you give me
a horse too. I'll take Daddy far away.
Someone will hide him for me."

"You're putting everyone at risk.
Your father, your mother, yourself.
And me. *Us.*"

I feel my temper rise
          and my need for justice
          over everything else.
"I'll talk to *Murphy*, then.
He'll get me a gun and a horse."
I march away from Johnny as fast as I can.

He rushes to catch up.
"We have to think this through.
We have to think of something
that will actually work."

"My father's set to die in five days.
Have you forgotten?
If he does,
I don't know what the world will look like.
Nothing will be the same.
I won't be the same."

"There's a boat leaving
for New York in two days," he tells me.
"One of Judge Grey's mistresses will be on it.
He can't have her parading
a belly around the town
when his wife is due for a visit."

"I'm ready for war," I say.
And I mean it.
I am sick of being trodden on,
of people with power
pushing everyone else around
and getting away with murder themselves.

"We have to get your father on to that boat too.
And just before it leaves,
so there'll be no dragging him back."

"And how are we meant to do that?" I ask.

Coffin Ships

"They're calling the boats
crossing the Atlantic coffin ships," Mammy says.
"Half the passengers on board are dying of disease.
I don't want to think of
your father's body being fired overboard."

"It's the only way, Mammy."

"And what about us?
Aren't we going with him?"

I hadn't thought about this.
Johnny and I didn't discuss it.

Letting Go

Johnny opens his hand
to show me a heavy metal
stamping seal.
I take it from him,
weigh it in my palm.

"How did you get it?" I ask.

"I went to see Judge Grey.
Told him I was in Killala
running an errand for my uncle.
We drank port and
he told me that Ireland could
lose several million people
and that it would be a blessing."

"He's like the devil himself."

"I wanted to crack open his skull."
He inhales through his nose.
"I'll write a letter and sign Grey's name
and wax-seal it with this.
When the guards receive it,
your father's sentence will be commuted to
transportation."

"To America?
And they're sending him on a cargo ship?
That doesn't happen."

"You think a redcoat will argue with Judge Grey?"

"What if they go to the judge to check?"

"In the middle of the night?"

"It won't work," I say.

Johnny straightens his waistcoat.
"It's the only way.
Anything else and there'd be blood.
I'll explain that Wicken will employ a local agent
to accompany your father."

I give him back the seal.
"My father's weak.
I'll have to take him to the port myself."

"No. You get your mother there.
Someone else will have to help him.
A man. A man the guards believe is an agent."

"Murphy," I say. "He has to help."
I drop my eyes. "And then what?"

Johnny hands me three pieces of paper:
tickets for passage to New York
on the *Oceanic Albert*.
"I'm not asking you to choose between me
and your family, Nell.
You have to go with them.

You'll die here.
My uncle will hunt you down
and make sure of it.
If he knows I helped, he'll kill me first."

"So that's it between us?"
I can hardly believe what he's saying,
         what he's planned.

"I want you alive, Nell.
Is that so much to ask?"

"You could come with us.
Buy a ticket and come with us.
Get away from him."

"If I leave now, my mother and sisters
will be destitute. I want you.
But I can't abandon them.
Especially not Helena."

"What about us?"

He unbuttons the cuffs of his shirt,
runs his hand through his hair.
"I'll come for you
when I have something
I can offer
that is more than just my love."

"Your love is enough," I say.

"Love is the reason I'm letting you go," he says.

Keepsake

"Can I have the figurines back?
The ones I carved of me and you?
I need them," he says.

I am shocked.
Saddened.

It is happening.

We are saying goodbye
and he needs a keepsake.

I take his hand and we walk
all the way to the bay,
where we scrounge for pieces of glass
among the stones.
I find a green bit,
smooth and no bigger than a pea.
He takes it from me.
"I need it," he says.

"I need you," I admit.

Thunderstorm

Johnny and I don't
cry about what's to come.

      We're out
in the thunder and lightning,
        dancing
cheek to cheek
        under the electric lights
with Mammy and Murphy
peeking out at us,
shaking their heads.

We're soaked through
and maybe we'll suffer with cold
in the morning.

We're surely risking a fever.

But it seems a shame to
waste the moment,
to waste the strange beauty
of that flashing, crashing, roaring
      rainstorm
when
tomorrow
we will be
      apart.

Green-Hearted

"I fixed them. See."
Johnny shows me the carvings,
      the boy and girl,
      him and me.
Grains of green glass
have been worked into the wood.

"Their hearts," I say.

"My heart," he says,
giving me the boy figurine,
"can stay with you."

"And yours," he says,
holding the girl to his own chest.
"This is where your heart should be."

He puts his arms around me
and my body feels
like it is being held together
with his arms,
      that my bones will shatter
      against the ground if
      he lets go,
that my soul itself
      will evaporate,
and I will
fall to

pieces
without him.
"You are a wonder, Nell Quinn," he whispers.

I inhale him one final time.
"John Browning," I say, and
without another breath
step away
and go to where
my mother is waiting.

The Last Thing

Mammy and I
lay some herbs
by the oak tree.

"Goodbye, son," Mammy says.

It is time to leave.

Johnny Waves Us Off

Johnny waves us off
but I cannot look back.

      I cannot.

Gangplank

We arrive at the port
cloaked in the darkness
of the deepest part of the night,
tired and footsore.

In my right hand,
a burlap bag
filled with rations
and the last of our possessions.
In my left,
Mammy's hand.

Up ahead
a man,
unmistakably my father,
waits on the dock
with his head bowed
so he will not be recognized.

I hardly believe it.
Johnny's plan worked?
The guards obeyed the forged letter
and let my father leave with Murphy.

I blink several times
to check it really is my father.

I expected no one, or
Judge Grey to be waiting,
his soldiers ready to arrest me.
I expected everything to go wrong,
like it has for so long now,
not a piece of luck anywhere
for anyone.

The guards will be in trouble.
For their stupidity.
For releasing a convicted criminal.

Mammy rushes to Daddy
as best her legs will allow
and slams against him.

I watch,
my feet stuck to the spot.
I touch the ground,
collect a stone from home.

Nightjars garland the ship,
stationed atop each mast.

"We're going to have a new life,"
Mammy tells me

when I shuffle to them,
as though the promise
of a new life
is a consolation
for what we are renouncing,
for what I am leaving behind.

And then we are boarding the boat,
trudging on to the already crowded deck,
men directing us to the bow.

Daddy kisses me.
"I knew you'd find a way," he says.
He hangs over the side and gazes into the
water sloshing against the ship.

"It wasn't me, Daddy.
It was Johnny," I say.
"I don't know how he managed it.
I feel like I'm dreaming.
You're really here?"

"What do you mean?" he asks.

I explain about the stolen seal
from Judge Grey,
about the letter that released my father.

"That was Johnny?"
My father looks aghast at my mother.

"What's wrong?' I ask.
"Daddy, what's happened?"

"They aren't finished with Wicken.
Murphy and the other men.
I warned Murphy against it.
Good God, the boy!"

"What are they going to do, Daddy?" I squeak.

"They're planning to murder
the landlord tonight."

I grab Mammy to keep from falling.
"Daddy! Johnny lives in that house.
They'll kill him too."

Daddy takes my arm to steady me.
"Murphy isn't wicked, Nell.
And it's Lord Wicken they're interested in."

"What will they do? Tell me, Daddy."

"I only know what Murphy told
me a few hours ago.
The men have had enough.
They plan to attack tonight."

I hold on to the railing and breathe quickly.
My knees eventually unable to hold me up,

I land on the wooden deck.
"Nell?" Mammy crouches next to me.

"I can't leave him," I murmur.
"I know you need me. But I can't."

"Nell . . ." Daddy takes my chin,
makes me look at him.
"Johnny can take care of himself."

"They'll hurt him. I know they will.
He's to inherit that land.
They'll kill him just for that."

"Be calm, Nell, please," Mammy says softly,
and starts to cry,
wiping the tears away quickly
with her sleeve.
"We have only you."

"Please, Nell," Daddy says quietly.

"You told me to take risks, Daddy.
I can't risk him dying
when I could save him.
I have to get off this ship.
I have to. I'm sorry."

Mammy gasps and wraps
herself around me so tightly
I feel the pattering of her heartbeat.

The gangplank creaks.
"I have to get off!" I screech.

A horn sounds.
Gulls caw and flap
though it is pitch black
and they should be asleep.

Mammy leans into me one final time,
but gently now.
"Run," she says. "Run."

Heartbreak

The sails on the ship
wave farewell
as the boat is unhooked
from the dock
     and sets sail
to a place
so far away
it is beyond imagining.

The Mob

A mob of men surround The Big House
with bottles, torches, and axes.
Some of them are carrying guns.

But it is completely silent,
each of them waiting for the order
to strike.

I run.

I dash toward the house, but before I reach it
a command rises out of the fog
and the men charge,
those with burning rushes
smashing windows with their elbows
and casting the flames through them.

A man escapes through the front door
and I wonder what he has done inside,
whether Lord Wicken
and the others are already dead,
their throats slit as they slept.

I run again,
and out of the haze
Murphy appears,
a gun across

his back, his face scored
    with soot.
"What the hell
are you doing here?"
He seizes my arm
and drags me with him.
"The servants were warned.
They're leaving by the back door.
You have to come with me."

"Johnny's inside.
You're murdering him!" I scream.

Murphy stares back at The Big House,
fire licking its bricks,
and seems to remember
that Lord Wicken isn't the only
inhabitant.
                John Browning
                lives there too.
                The boy who saved my father.

Murphy lets me go.
"You're on your own, Nell."

The Dresser

I race through the house
        and up the stairs,
though the smoke is blinding.

Johnny is collapsed
        in a heap
                on the landing.

I shake him. "Johnny! Johnny!"
and he rouses himself.

"My uncle is trapped," he wheezes.

He points along the hallway.

A door is ajar and I hear it then:
Lord Wicken crying out
for someone to save him
because his way has been barred:
a dresser pushed against
the door to prevent him from leaving.

On my hands and knees
I crawl the length of the hallway,
try with every ounce of strength
to push the dresser aside.
But it is as though
it has been filled with bricks.

It is immovable.

My eyes sting
and in every direction
I look
there are flames.

Even the rugs have caught fire.

I cannot do any more.

Gone

I drag Johnny down the stairs
and outside, where we collapse
on to the gravel driveway.

He is weak.
Cannot speak.

Maggie Kennedy runs toward us.
"Child," she says.
"Master Browning. Praise God."
She is back moments later
with a tin cup of water, dribbling it
between Johnny's lips.

Silas Simmons and the other
servants stand over us.
Hours ago I would have pounced on Silas.
Now, I realize,
he is nothing to me
and he has nothing left.

Johnny sits up a little.
"My uncle," he says.

"He's gone, son," Maggie tells him.

And

I do not know
how to feel about
Wicken's death.

I do not think I feel
a thing.

I'll Love You

Redcoats turn over the ashes,
looking for evidence of life.

Johnny says,
"The land your father and grandfather tended
for all those years will be yours now, Nell.
I want you to have it."

"I want that, but I also . . ."
I step back so we can look at each other.

He suddenly sees my pain.
And that I have no more fight.

"You want to leave," he guesses.

"I can't stay here after everything."

"What if *I'm* here?
Is there nothing for you then?"

"Johnny." I am crying too hard to reply.

We have to find a way out.

> This place, these fields
> are no longer Home.

Everything that once grew green is rotten.

"Then we'll go," he says.
"We'll go wherever we have to."

Away

The cloth of daybreak reaches across the sky.
The road ahead is rocky and uneven.

Johnny kisses my wrist,
the center of my palm,
my lips.

I hold his hand
and find,
in my pocket,
with the other hand,
the carving of him.

They can be together now,
whether they survive this disaster or not.

Wherever they find themselves,
those little carvings,
those tiny green hearts,
they can be together now.

The End
and the Beginning

My Heart

It is hard to tell a love story
and also the story of a people
being torn apart.

But this is what happened in 1846
when the blight came to Ireland
and Johnny along with it:
I fell in love
when everything
around me
       fell
       down.

       I look back
       at the ruin
       and the pain
       with guilt
       and sorrow,
with a gnawing ache
to have returned to me
all that was taken,
with anger about the beauty
that could have been saved.

But I look back
with hope too.

Because there is beauty still.

My father and mother found
each other
again.

Johnny and I found
each other too.

It is true
that love wins
and also that
evil sometimes
wins as well.

But the
inheritance
of love cannot be
overstated:
the things
that can blossom
from it . . .

When I am sad
or lonely
for the people
I have lost,
I am quiet
and let love

guide them
back to me.

I usually find them.

I usually find them
        hidden within
        myself,
concealed quietly
in the safety
of my own heart.

Acknowledgments

Huge thanks to The Arts Council of Ireland for their bursary, which significantly contributed to the completion of this novel, particularly Sarah Bannan, Aoife Moynihan, Orla Casey, and Audrey Keane.

Thank you to Fin Dwyer for his historical insights and for going through this book with a sharp eye and fine-tooth comb. Furthermore, his *Irish History Podcast* was an invaluable resource.

The following books informed my understanding of the Great Hunger and the culture in Ireland at the time, and I am grateful to the authors for their vigorous research: Christine Kinealy's *This Great Calamity: The Irish Famine 1845–52* (1994); Cecil Woodham-Smith's *The Great Hunger: Ireland 1845–1849* (1962); Tim Pat Coogan's *The Famine Plot: England's Role in Ireland's Greatest Tragedy* (2012); Ciarán Ó Murchadha's *The Great Famine: Ireland's Agony 1845–1852* (2011); and Susan Campbell Bartoletti's *Black Potatoes: The Story of the Great Irish Famine, 1845–1850* (2001).

Thank you to Rebecca McNally, Fliss Stevens, Beatrice Cross, and the whole team at Bloomsbury Publishing for their hard work on this novel, and to Zöe Griffiths, who began the complex journey of recrafting the story with me many years ago.

Thank you to Martha Mihalick and the Greenwillow team for taking this story across the pond.

Thank you to Julia Churchill and everyone else who holds my hand at A.M. Heath.

For reasons too complicated to go into, this novel has taken twelve years to complete. The following people and organizations have been there along the way and are due immeasurable gratitude for their ongoing support: Children's Books Ireland, Words Ireland, Poetry Ireland, Booktrust Northern Ireland, Booktrust, The National Literacy Trust, CLPE, Andreas Michalitsianos, Richard Crossan, Daniel Crossan, Kevin Crossan, Jimmy Fox, Nicola Speers, Ilia Apostolopoulou, Gráinne Clear, Zareena Huber, Nikki Sheehan, Abie Longstaff, Phil Earle, Lisa Heathfield, Charlotte Hacking, Rick O'Shea, Elaina Ryan, Cecelia Ahern, John Boyne, Clare Nestor, Jordana Jacobs, Bernadette Larkin, Cormac Kinsella, Louise Dobbin, Ros Harding, Joy Court, Tricia Adams, Amy McKay, and Matthew Dench.

Thank you to August/Marcus Sedgwick. We lost a heavyweight in the book world in November 2022 and I lost my friend.

Thank you and I love you to Nancy Crossan. I wish you could read this with your busy pencil; you were the best at pointing out my mistakes and not making me feel bad about them. I miss you, Mama.

About the Author

Sarah Crossan has lived in Dublin, London, and New York, and now lives in East Sussex. She graduated with a degree in philosophy and literature before training as an English and drama teacher at the University of Cambridge. Sarah Crossan won the 2016 CILIP Carnegie Medal, the YA Book Prize, the CBI Book of the Year Award, and many other prizes for her novel *One*. *Moonrise* was shortlisted for the Costa Children's Book Award, the YA Book Prize, the CBI Book of the Year Award, and the CLiPPA Poetry Award. She was the Laureate na nÓg (Ireland's Children's Literature Laureate) from 2018–2020. Her novels have been translated into more than twenty-five languages.